DOG DAYS

Blossom squeezed under the fence and trotted across the Hughes' front lawn. The flagstone patio felt hot to her pads, but something irresistible propelled her forward. Her nose stopped at a still form lying on a beach towel. She touched the thing with her paw. It did not move. Edging her body next to it, she rubbed her back against it from end to end. Large black sunglasses fell to the ground with a clatter. Blind eyes stared up at the branches of a willow tree. The dog gave a tentative scratch with one stubby paw. When there was no response, she climbed on top of the thing and stared into sightless eyes. Finally, satisfied it was safe, Blossom rolled over. Paws in the air, she arched her back. Heaven! Digging her head into the lifeless flesh, she squirmed happily, wriggling like a snake until, exhausted, she scrambled down and trotted happily home.

★

NANCY BELL

RESTORED TO DEATH

WORLDWIDE®

TORONTO • NEW YORK • LONDON
AMSTERDAM • PARIS • SYDNEY • HAMBURG
STOCKHOLM • ATHENS • TOKYO • MILAN
MADRID • WARSAW • BUDAPEST • AUCKLAND

RESTORED TO DEATH

A Worldwide Mystery/June 2004

First published by St. Martin's Press LLC.

ISBN 0-373-26496-8

Printed in U.S.A.

RESTORED
TO
DEATH

ONE

"YOU'RE ATTICUS," said Patty.

"What?" Jackson looked up with a start from the Sunday paper he'd been reading.

"Atticus," his daughter repeated. "You're Atticus, and I'm Scout." She tilted the library book she'd been reading toward him.

"Ah," he said, *"To Kill a Mockingbird.* I never read that book, but as I recall, your mother really liked the movie. I think she had a secret crush on Gregory Peck." He smiled fondly at his daughter, who sat sprawled across the wicker porch swing, all elbows and knees, her dark curly hair tumbling around her shoulders. His sister-in-law Dora, always Johnny-on-the-spot with unsolicited advice, had just the other day suggested that he make her get it cut. Never, he thought. It was fine healthy hair, and Patty liked it the way it was. He would have to defy Dora on this one. After Jackson's wife died two years ago, Dora had bombarded him with her own theories on child-raising. Jackson knew she meant well, but, since she was childless herself, he had a feeling she wasn't the best one to be giving out parenting advice. Mostly, he just smiled and ignored her.

"What's the book about?" he asked, unwrapping a Don Diego cigar and sniffing it appreciatively.

"About a single daddy who's also a *lawyer,* raising a daughter. They live in a small town just like *we* do. Scout, that's a *girl* in case you didn't know, has a brother and they get into all *kinds* of adventures while the daddy defends a colored man that's accused of a crime, but didn't do it. It's a very grown-up book." She looked up at Jackson. "Don't worry, Daddy, Miss Perkins *said* we could read it for *credit.*" She slung one leg over the back of the swing and returned to her book, a tiny frown creasing her forehead.

Since Patty had arrived at that never-never land between childhood and adolescence, she rarely spoke without emphasis. Jackson smiled. "Where are your glasses? You're squinting."

Patty wriggled around until she could get her hand into the pocket of her shorts. She pulled out a pair of glasses and stuck them on her face. "Yuk. I *hate* these things."

"Bet you can see better, though."

"Umm." She was once again lost in her book.

Jackson got up and stretched, then walked over to the porch railing to admire the view of his neighborhood. The September sun bathed Hackberry Street in a golden haze so that the turn-of-the-century houses seemed to take on a brand-new refinement—even Old Man Hogaboom's bungalow on the corner, which hadn't seen a paintbrush in forty years. In the yard across the street, sunbeams filtered through the trees and cast moving shadows on the copper coat of Shandy, the Boyds' Irish setter, who was napping under a mimosa tree. Just then, Shandy's owner, Ham Boyd, came out of his house wearing green plaid Bermuda shorts and a yellow polo shirt. He stood for a moment admiring his yard, then grinned and waved at Jackson as he bent to pick up the hose and give it a sharp tug, causing the attached sprinkler to tumble across the turf to a new spot.

Indian summer was in full swing in Post Oak, Texas (pop. 5,387), and soon folks would be storing away the hoses and sprinklers and hauling out the bushel baskets and leaf rakes. Jackson could almost smell the burning leaves and his neighbors' honest sweat. He frowned as he looked at his own yard. His wife's prize azaleas drooped against the iron fence begging for water, while the wisteria beside the porch snaked happily around the downspout and up onto the roof. His lawn was a field of dandelions, their seed balls bobbing like soap bubbles in the breeze. He would have to see about getting Willie Bee Scott to come around and pull things together.

The place had gone to seed since Gretchen died. Jackson smiled, thinking of his feisty little wife. He missed her. She had been only thirty-seven when the doctors diagnosed leukemia. She died eighteen months to the day later. After six months of confusion and grief, Jackson and Patty had settled into a comfortable, if haphazard routine, barely noticing the house and yard. Jackson had hired Lutie Faye Ivory to come in five days a week to fix meals and do laundry. On weekends, they were left to fend for themselves.

Jackson flipped his spent cigar over the porch rail.

He stretched and yawned. "Think I'll have a nap," he said. "How about walking down to the café for some supper after I get up?"

Patty flicked an assenting finger his way, not taking her eyes from her book....

JACKSON AND PATTY walked over cracked and buckled sidewalks to the Wagon Wheel Café, which sat square in the middle of the block. Even on its best days Post Oak was not an attractive town. On Sunday evening, when the streets were deserted, it was downright depressing, what with cast-off papers hugging the gutters and little cyclones of dust rising up in the middle of the street. The one traffic light at the intersection of Main and Franklin only blinked yellow.

Post Oak was settled in the mid-nineteenth century and remained much the same sleepy farming community for ninety years. It had been reborn during the East Texas oil boom of the thirties, its streets teeming with hustlers and roughnecks hoping to make a quick buck. For a few short years, the promise of easy money had lifted the spirits of depression-weary locals as well. Lease hounds occupied every street corner on Saturday afternoons, promising riches to farmers who were only too willing to sign over their mineral rights for pennies an acre. A few locals made money; most did not and had to stand by and watch their land cut to shreds by rutty roads leading to huge, stinking drilling rigs that spewed forth foul smoke and not much more. Still, for a while little Post Oak reveled in the dream before the oil dried up and the town settled back into sun-baked inertia.

At the end of the block, the residential area gave way to commercial, and the pair walked past the Wag 'n' Bag, which this week sported triangular plastic streamers extending from the square brick building to the two gas pumps out front. Newspaper racks by the door contained the *Dallas Morning News* and the *Post Oak Sentinel*. Signs in the windows advertised ice cream bars, Miller beer, and Mrs. Baird's bread. Several boys with bikes lingered near the Coke machine, talking loudly and glancing obliquely at Patty.

"I hate when they do that," she said.

"Isn't that Sonny Smart?"

"I really didn't notice." She tossed her head.

Inside, the Wagon Wheel was bright with fluorescent light and smelling of potatoes frying. The walls were painted green, now stained from years of grease and smoke. The counter stools and chair seats were covered with green pearlescent plastic. Rip Riggins, the owner, had recently installed a brand-new frozen custard machine behind the counter.

The place was almost empty when Jackson and Patty arrived. The only other patrons were the Haygood brothers, Bob and Bill, who sat hunched over mugs of coffee at the counter. Bob was trying to tell a joke to Muriel, the waitress.

"That ain't the way it went, brother," Bill said. "You see, this monkey tells the bartender—"

"Who's tellin' this story?" Bob said. "Now shut up before you give away the punch line. See, the monkey was wearin' a tuxedo, but there wasn't no hole for his tail to hang through...."

"Booth or table?" Jackson asked, holding the screen door open for Patty.

"Booth, so I can play the jukebox."

"Hidy, Judge, hidy, Patty," said the red-haired Muriel, slapping menus down in front of them. "Need time to look?"

Jackson put his hand down flat on top of his menu. "You know what I want."

"T-bone steak, medium, french fries, small salad with bleu and coffee. Apple pie for dessert. How about you, Patty?"

Patty was already squinting at the chrome jukebox attached to the wall. "Cheeseburger and fries, mayonnaise, no mustard, cut the onions. Daddy, have you got some quarters?"

While Patty stuffed quarters into the jukebox, Jackson observed his all-too-familiar surroundings. The place hadn't changed one whit since his youth when he and his friends would stop by after school for a cold drink before going home. Grease- and smoke-stained, the suspended ceiling hung low over the row of green plastic booths that hugged the wall opposite the counter. In a line down the center of the room stood three oilcloth-covered tables, each bearing the usual napkin dispensers, bottles of catsup, and metal-capped salt and pepper shakers. Underfoot, the black and white hexagon-shaped ceramic tiles attested to the fact that the building itself was quite old and had, in fact, started life as a bank.

Muriel shouted their orders to Rip back in the kitchen, then came back and slid into the green plastic booth beside Jackson. "You doing okay?"

She had asked that every single day since his wife died.

"Fine," he said, just like always. "Only I wish the women in this town would quit trying to fix me up. Last Thursday, Mimi Thorsell asked me over to dinner and, wouldn't you know it, her old college roommate just happened to be visiting from Florida."

"Well?"

Jackson opened his paper napkin and spread it in front of him on the table, smoothing it with his hands. "She was nice enough, but not my type." Jackson was always careful not to bad-mouth the ladies he was introduced to. "I just wish they'd leave us alone. Patty and I are doing just fine."

"It's a woman's job," Muriel said. "If there's anything we can't stand, it's a happy bachelor."

"What about you?" Jackson asked. "Joe been bothering you anymore?"

"Not too much." Muriel got busy with her order pad, which was empty except for Jackson's order.

"Muriel"—he looked at her severely—"if he violates his restraining order, we can have the sheriff pick him up."

"No. It's okay. Uh-oh, there comes Mr. and Mrs. Rice. They'll be wanting one meal with two plates, like always. That old man's so tight he squeaks. Look at her; she gets frailer every day. Well, I'd better go get their order."

The old man, tall, well-muscled, and broad-shouldered, wore a shiny suit, a white shirt, and a black bow tie. His shoulder blades protruded only slightly against the black of his jacket, and his hands hung, spotted and slightly gnarled, from frayed white cuffs. He had a shock of white hair of a coarse texture that would forever resist efforts to tame it. The woman was tiny—so tiny, in fact, that it was difficult to imagine she could maintain her footing should she be caught in a windstorm. She wore a cotton house-dress, neatly pressed, but faded almost white from so much washing. She was pale as a porcelain plate and bent almost double with osteoporosis.

Muriel spoke briefly with the old couple, then opened the pie case and took out one slice of apple pie. She put the pie down between them and set a small plate and fork in front of each.

Jackson observed the two. "It's a shame," he said to nobody in particular as he watched them meticulously divide the pie in half.

"Look at them. Haven't had a decent meal in thirty years, I'll bet!" Muriel slid back into the booth next to Jackson. "Somebody ought to do something: *You* ought to do something, Jackson."

"Me? Why me?"

"You're the county judge, aren't you? It's your job to see that women don't starve to death because they're married to a mean old miser that won't even buy food enough to keep a ladybug alive." Muriel warmed to her subject. "Hell, he's the richest man in town. What about Ray Junior? Does he know this is going on?"

"Nobody knows where he is," Jackson said. "I'll drop by the human services office and have a chat with Eunice. Maybe they have the authority to look into it. I don't know what else I can do."

Just then Rip rang the huge cowbell he used to let Miriam know when orders were ready. Miriam left the table and returned with their food.

"Sit down and keep us company while we eat," Jackson shouted over Patty's jukebox selections.

"Can't," she replied. "Rip's been a regular old bear since Doc changed his blood pressure medicine. He says I've got to clean out the fryer while business is slow. I think he's depressed. I seen on *20-20* where... Oh, Lordy, look at poor Mrs. Rice!"

The old lady was rising from her chair, clutching her throat, eyes wide with terror. She opened her mouth, but no sound came out.

"Do something, Jackson." Muriel clutched his arm. "She's turning black!"

Before anyone had time to move, Patty scooted out of the booth and got behind Mrs. Rice, yanking her out of her chair. She wrapped her arms around the woman's waist and pushed her fists hard into her midsection once, twice, three times. Suddenly Mrs. Rice coughed, and a bit of pie flew out of her mouth.

Patty eased her back into the chair, then looked at her father with an expression of pure astonishment. "It works! I never thought that old Heimlich maneuver would really work. Daddy, did you see that?"

Jackson beamed with pride. "I sure did, honey."

"Where'd you ever learn to do that?" Muriel asked in amazement.

"At camp last summer," Patty said. "We all had to take the lifesaving class. I never thought I'd have to use it."

"We're all proud of you," Jackson said, giving her a quick hug.

Mr. Rice looked at her and nodded, then bent over his wife. "Are you all right, Myrtice? That's a girl, give me a big smile, then. Brace up, old girl. You're a strong one."

Mrs. Rice tried. One side of her mouth started to make its way in a northerly direction but couldn't seem to gain much momentum. Just then, Rip's cat, Fluffy, wandered out of the kitchen to see what all the commotion was about and, hoping for a game, rolled over on her back, wrapped her front paws around the woman's ankle, and kicked vigorously with her back legs. Mrs. Rice crumpled against her husband in a dead faint.

By now the Haygood brothers and Rip had joined the little circle around the table. Everyone had an opinion as to what should be done.

"Lay her down on the floor."

"Put her head between her legs."

"Somebody call Doc Sample."

"No, call 911."

"We ain't *got* 911."

"*No.* Gracious, no!" Mr. Rice knew full well what pirates doctors could be. "She's coming around. I'll just take her home as soon as she feels strong enough for the walk."

Muriel brought out a towel dipped in ice water and folded it against the woman's forehead. In a moment, her eyelids fluttered open. After she had rested a bit and drunk a few sips of water, it was decided that Bob and Bill would drive her home in their Camaro.

As they started for the door, Mr. Rice paused and turned back.

"By the way, Muriel," he said. "Do you think it would be possible for us to have a small container? Myrtice hardly touched her pie."

AFTER EVERYBODY LEFT, Patty holding a double frozen custard cone, Muriel locked the front door, then reversed the cardboard sign hanging in the window so the *Closed* side faced the sidewalk. Wearily, she walked back to the kitchen, where she was relieved to see that Rip had already inserted the drain fitting into the deep fryer and begun to empty the used oil into a plastic bucket.

"I was going to do that," she said.

An expression close to tenderness crossed Rip's weather-beaten features. "I got it. You get on them dishes."

"You sure?"

Rip closed the spigot on the fryer, then lifted the bucket of rancid oil and headed for the back door. "Might' near done now."

Muriel nodded and turned to the big square commercial dishwasher standing next to a deep stainless steel sink. She was grateful it was Sunday and the pile of dishes was mercifully small. She rinsed the plates and glasses and placed them in the green plastic trays, which she inserted through a door on the sink side of the dishwasher. Next she filled the machine and pressed the start button, watching to make sure the correct amount of chemicals dripped into the receptacle on the side. In two minutes, the dishes were clean. She removed them from an identical door on the opposite side and left them to drain until morning. She was wiping her hands on a paper towel when Rip came back into the kitchen.

"How 'bout a Coke?" He removed his soiled apron and tossed it into a basket in the corner.

Muriel followed Rip into the café and sat in a booth while he opened two diet Cokes and brought them to the table. "I got something stronger if you want it," he said.

Muriel shook her head, then bent down and untied the thick-soled oxfords she had ordered out of a restaurant supply catalog. She slipped one foot out of its shoe and massaged it gently.

"Dogs barkin', are they?"

Muriel nodded.

"Stick 'um over here. I'll rub 'um for you."

"Thanks, Rip." Gratefully, she removed both shoes and propped her stockinged feet onto the opposite seat.

She sighed and sipped her Coke while Rip's callused hands worked the soreness away.

At forty-two, Muriel showed her age and more. Furthermore, she did little to disguise it. Red hair, now streaked with gray, was washed weekly, then left to dry and hang loosely around her shoulders. She was one of those women who, at middle age, begin to thicken noticeably around the waist and hips. Now her skimpy uniforms strained across her broad behind. Her acne-scarred face was large and square. It would have escaped notice except for those startling tur-

quoise eyes and large white teeth. Muriel smiled often
and for some reason, men found her alluring.

Rip loved her hopelessly and had suffered agonies
on the days she came to work with bruises and cuts
inflicted by her husband. He was relieved when she
finally left the man and swore out a restraining order
against him. Still, Rip didn't trust the law much, so
every night before bedtime he drove past her house
just in case.

Rip had begun to believe that protecting Muriel
was a Holy Cause, a state of affairs Muriel found
perplexing. Only last Monday, he had overheard a
conversation between three oil field workers in this
very booth. Muriel had just taken their orders and
gone behind the counter to get their coffee.

How'd you like a piece of that?

*Me? Man, I'd have her yellin' for her mama. That
old gal wouldn't never know what hit her.*

Yeah, right. You and how many others?

*I don't need no help, man. I'd fuck her till her hat
flew off.*

*Reckon you can both forget it. Old Ron Hughes
done beat you to the punch.*

*Him? That little sissy. Hell, on my worst day, I
could outfuck him.*

*Oh, yeah? Well, I could… Oh, hey, Rip. We was
just—*

Git out!

Muriel had only stared in bewilderment when Rip
tossed them all out on the street and told them what
would happen if they ever came back.

TWO

BROTHER STEVE LARGENT adjusted the hot water a millimeter to the left so the water was just a fraction warmer than the drinking water his wife kept in the refrigerator. Now it was perfect. It didn't do to take a hot shower even on the coldest of winter mornings. It slowed the blood and made one sluggish for the rest of the day. He lathered his hair with Prell, then replaced the lid on the plastic bottle before returning it to its spot in the little wire basket hung over the shower head. He himself had installed it, hoping to maintain some semblance of order in the bathroom that he shared with his wife, Vanessa. After toweling dry and returning the towel to the bar, folded so the corners were straight, he took a moment to admire his naked body in the mirror. For pushing forty, he was pleased with what he saw, not an ounce of fat and very little chest hair to mar the perfection of his physique. That kind of shape was what came from playing racquetball at the high school gym every Wednesday and Saturday without fail. For a moment, pulling up his boxer shorts, he wondered how he'd look in a bright orange Speedo. Then, remembering that pride is the deadliest of all the sins, he quickly turned his hand to the job of shaving. Afterward, he rinsed the lavatory and dried it with a hand towel until it shone. He shook his head ruefully as he glanced at the identical sink to his right, his wife's. The bowl was full of rollers, and he thought he saw a gelatinous bar of soap under them. Face powder dusted the whole thing, and an open lipstick had rolled over on its side, leaving a trail of vermilion across the porcelain. He gingerly removed each roller from the sink and replaced them on their electric holder, then, using a washcloth, removed the soap and tossed it into the trash. Carefully, he raised the chrome stopper from its position and winced as a trail of hair and soap slime came with it. He dropped it back in place and wondered if it would do a scrap of good to counsel her again about cleanliness being next to godliness. The last time he had made an attempt at this, she had grabbed his head and nibbled his ear until he forgot all about cleanliness or godliness.

After dressing in a blue suit, black socks, and white oxford cloth shirt, which he carefully removed from a dry cleaner's bag, he selected a blue tie with a pattern of tiny red diamonds. He stole one last satisfied glance at himself, then made his way downstairs singing, ''There is a fountain filled with blood, drawn from Emmanuel's veins.''

''SO I TOLD HIM, I said, 'Get that ding-blasted alternator off my dining room table, or you're sleeping on the couch till hell freezes over.' 'Course, he don't give a good goddam—oops, sorry—on account of he ain't been interested in *you know* since 'long about '78 or '9.'' Edna Buchannan set Jackson's coffee down on his desk with a bang. "Hell, he'd just as soon lay on that ratty old sofa and go to sleep with the TV going."

Jackson lit a Don Diego, his second of the day, and emptied the ashtray into a metal wastebasket beside his desk.

"Edna, I wish you'd—"

"I know. Clean up my language. Well, if you had to live with that old fart, you'd cuss, too."

Jackson had to admit, she had a point. Orville Buchannan was as sorry as they came, and without Edna's small salary from the county, he guessed the two of them would have to go on welfare. He remembered Edna from high school. She had been one year ahead of him and valedictorian of her graduating class. She had been popular with the boys, with her curly blond hair that refused to stay under the headbands she wore and tended to escape into soft curls over her forehead. Her eyes were blue and her skin the color of cream. Mrs. Martin, the senior English teacher, had wangled a scholarship for her at a nearby state college, but her father, who could see nothing to be gained from higher education, had made her go to work at the dime store the day after graduation. It was while Jackson was away at law school that she married Orville Buchannan and learned to swear like a sailor. As soon as he hung out his shingle, Jackson hired her to work for him and trained her as a legal secretary. She had never once let him down.

"Hell, I wouldn't care so much, only his mama and them are coming for dinner on Saturday. Well, you know that old woman never did think much of me."

Edna's big hair shook with indignation. "I'd hate for her to walk in and find that thing spread all over the table where we're supposed to eat!"

Jackson hated himself but had to ask. "Why does he have an alternator on the dining room table?"

She folded her arms and glared at him. "He's rebuilding the son-of-a-bitch. Thinks it'll make that pile of junk he calls a truck run better.... Oh, hi, Mr. Rice. Come on in. I'll just go pour you a cup of coffee."

Ray Rice, Sr., stood awkwardly just inside the office door holding a gift-wrapped box. "I hope I'm not intruding. Perhaps I should have telephoned first."

"Not at all." Jackson gestured toward one of the two leather client's chairs opposite his desk.

The old man sank into the chair and nodded thanks to Edna, who had set a mug of coffee in front of him. He placed the package carefully on the desk and picked up the mug. Jackson noticed that his hand trembled as he brought the cup to his lips.

"My wife sends heartfelt thanks to your little daughter. She saved her life, of course."

"That's nice, but you didn't—"

"No, no. Not at all. We are in debt to her. Perhaps this will help even the score."

Jackson picked up the package. It was wrapped in much-used tissue paper and topped with a bow that must have seen more than a few Christmas mornings.

"I'll see she gets it. And thanks."

Mr. Rice rose as if to leave, then sank back down into his chair. "Er, there's one other thing, Judge Crain. My wife and I have a dilemma. We thought you might be able to help. It's a matter of the utmost discretion. Myrtice and I talked it over and decided you were the man for the job—in your capacity as county judge, of course.''

Jackson nodded, fully understanding the old man's meaning. He meant this consultation was in no way addressed to Jackson Crain, fee-charging practicing attorney.

Roy Rice leaned forward and lowered his voice. ''You see, someone is trying to kill us.''

Jackson leaned forward. ''Why don't you tell me about it.''

''There's not much to tell. Someone's trying to kill my wife and myself and I want protection under the law. Young man, in my career, I've paid more taxes than anyone in this county. Now I want my money's worth.'' The old man's hands began to shake uncontrollably. He hastily hid them in his lap.

''I understand your feelings in the matter. Now, what's happened to make you think you and Mrs. Rice are in danger?''

''We are being spied upon. Day and night someone is watching our house.''

Jackson nodded. ''Go on.''

''They have even come in the house—at night while we're sleeping. Myrtice heard them only last night walking around on the third floor.''

''And did you investigate?''

''The next morning. When I went up to the room, nothing had been disturbed. Still, Myrtice is not a hysterical woman. If she says she heard something, she heard something.''

''What did it sound like?''

"Like, well, I can only tell you what Myrtice said. She, well…she said it sounded like someone was playing marbles up there."

"And did you hear it?"

"No, sir, I didn't. I'm…er…a little hard of hearing, you see. Have been for quite some time." He crossed his legs and rested both hands on his knee. "I have seen something, however, outside the kitchen window, a form standing in the shadows. Sometimes we feel that someone is watching us. I know, I know, it's only a feeling, but taken with the other evidence I've given you, you should feel more than justified in alerting the sheriff to keep a close watch on our property."

Jackson humored the man. "I'll certainly see that it's done, Mr. Rice. Now you go home and tell your wife not to worry anymore." Jackson stood. "And thanks on Patty's behalf for the gift. I'll take it to her when I go home for lunch."

Mr. Rice got to his feet. "I do feel relieved," he said. "Now, you are sure you'll talk to the sheriff?"

"Absolutely," Jackson said, following the old man to the door. "Good-bye, sir. Oh, I almost forgot something." He took a slip of paper from his pocket and thrust it in Jackson's hand. "This was slipped under our back door. Myrtice found it when she went in to cook breakfast."

When the old man left, Jackson pushed open the door to the adjoining office, where Edna sat at her computer feigning interest in the rows of figures that made up the county road budget.

"Well, what did you think?" he asked.

"Huh? What do I think about what?"

"You know what I mean. I saw the light blinking on the intercom the whole time."

"Hell, I couldn't hear nothin'," she said. "All I heard was your side. Anyway, you could of punched the button." Edna spun around in her chair until she faced him. "The old geezer seemed scared—of something besides having to spend a penny of his precious cash."

"He didn't have much to go on," Jackson said, striking a match and holding it to the end of his now-cold cigar. "Still, he honestly believes somebody is after him and his wife. The old man was scared—that was obvious."

"Shi—heck, Jackson. He didn't tell you nothing. Anybody can start imagining things if they let themselves. Hell, I do it myself sometimes when my old man's off somewhere."

Jackson moved a stack of papers off the chair next to her desk and sat down. "But just suppose they're not imagining it. Who would want to hurt a harmless old couple?"

Edna raised an eyebrow at him. "Jackson, you stay stuck in some ivory tower somewhere. How about one of the folks that he stole their farm from? He's got property all over this county that he's loaned money on and then foreclosed." She leaned in close. "And how about just about any farmer in this town he ever bought cotton from? Ever'body knows his old scales weighed two hundred pounds light. Ever pick two hundred pounds of cotton, Jackson? Them folks, my own daddy was one, worked from can till can't over that cotton, and he cheated each and every one."

"That's ancient history, Edna. We haven't had a cotton crop in this county for forty years."

"People don't forget something like that," she said. "You mark my words. Somebody—lots of somebodies—have a bone to pick with that old crook."

Jackson frowned. "He says somebody's been hanging around the house. They've heard sounds coming from the ballroom on the third floor. It's not been used since Ray Junior was in high school. We used to go up there and play pool when we were kids."

"What kind of sounds?"

Jackson grinned. "He said it sounded like someone was playing marbles up there."

"Could be squirrels. Once, me and Orville had 'um in our attic. Hell, it sounded like they was a bowling alley right over our heads. What it was, was pecans rolling across the floor. Still and all, it's a stretch goin' from strange noises to somebody wantin' to kill them. What else did he say?"

Jackson walked back into his office and returned carrying a wrinkled slip of paper. "He found this shoved under the back door," he said.

Edna took the paper and squinted at it. "What the hell is this supposed to be?" she asked.

"What do you think?"

"Looks like a boat floatin' in the water to me. What do you think?"

"Could be a skull and crossbones—drawn by a first-grader." Jackson put the paper in his jacket pocket. "I guess I'll just step over to the sheriff's

office right now with this. He may want to tell whoever's on night duty to patrol the house every hour
or so.'' Jackson stood and started toward the door.
''Maybe I'll just drop by the house and visit with the
two of them later this week.''

THE SIGN FROM the Maverick Market on the highway
above the house made irregular patterns on the wall
of the tiny bedroom. The roar of traffic, punctuated
occasionally by police sirens, the persistent throbbing
of a boom box in the next block, and the apneic
snores of the man sleeping in the next room perme-
ated the space with dissonant sound. Boogie never
noticed. It was as much a part of her world as the
muddy ditch that ran alongside the road or the stray
dogs that foraged the garbage cans at night. Curled
into a tight ball under the sheet, she tried to make
herself as small as possible, just another, somewhat
larger lump in the center of an already lumpy mat-
tress. He was gone finally, and she lay trembling with
impotent rage. The putrid smell of him—rotting teeth,
stale beer, and an unwashed body—refused to be ex-
orcised. She knew, for she had tried. Once, after he
left, she had stood in the shower for an hour, letting
the water run until it was icy cold, and scrubbed with
soap until her skin was red and tingling. The smell
had stayed on. She was afraid it was part of her now
and would never go away.

Boogie waited. She knew the routine. Her grandmother would be passed out in her recliner chair in
the living room, the television still on. She knew he
had intentionally pressed drinks, vodka and orange

juice, on her until she lost consciousness before coming into Boogie's room. At first his visits had been sporadic, maybe once every week or two. She had tried to fight him off once, but he slapped her hard across the face, then pressed his forearm across her chest so forcefully, she thought she would pass out from lack of air. Lately, he had come every night, grunting and humping until he was finished, then rolling off the bed and leaving without a word. She listened until she heard the bedsprings creak in the next room and heard his snores. Then she knew he would sleep through the night.

Slowly, Boogie stretched her legs and moved to the edge of the bed. She quickly dressed in shorts and a T-shirt and retrieved her school backpack from underneath the bed. Her ninth-grade books and papers had been removed and stashed in a drawer. Now the canvas bag contained a change of clothes, a wide-toothed comb, her toothbrush, a small plastic makeup kit, and her most priceless possession, a photo of her as a baby held by the mother she didn't remember. It was creased and faded and had been taken at the beach at Rockport. Boogie knew that because she recognized the pier in the background.

She opened the door that led from her bedroom to the living room and, stepping carefully around her grandmother's recliner, eased herself out the front door. At the end of the block she waited until a black, low-slung car pulled up to the curb. Without glancing back, she got into the car.

''Drive,'' she said.

THREE

DORA HUGHES WALKED out to her Spanish-tiled patio at six-thirty sharp, trainers in hand. Standing almost six feet tall, she would have been an imposing woman except for the slight stoop of her shoulders and the way her large head thrust forward like that of a vulture. Her hair, dark and lustrous, was pulled back from her angular face with a plain rubber band. This simple hairstyle only served to highlight her prominent Roman nose and deep-set hazel eyes. She seated herself on the edge of the wrought-iron settee and pulled on the shoes. Dora didn't notice the sun rising over the golf course, nor did she glance at the family of cottontail rabbits feeding on the seventh green. Her thoughts were fixed on her morning run and whether she could beat yesterday's time of fifty minutes for the three-mile course. She fitted a sweatband around her forehead and completed her prerun stretches before setting off into the stillness of the morning.

The run would clear her mind, she thought. Then she'd go back to her spotless kitchen, make a pot of tea, and plan what to do about Ron and the bombshell he'd dropped last night.

Dora had been making supper when he strolled into the kitchen and made himself a scotch. Then, instead of going back into the den to watch the news, he had plunked himself down at the breakfast bar to have his drink.

Dora stopped chopping celery to look at him.

"Dora, we need to talk."

"Ron, can't you see I'm—"

"I know. You're busy. Why do you always have to be— No, never mind. That's not important now."

That was when he had told her about Muriel, told her that he had fallen suddenly and hopelessly in love for the first time in his life, that he never knew he could feel this way about a woman. She remembered how his eyes had gone soft when he spoke of the woman's great big heart and the way she seemed to anticipate his every need without him having to tell her. He had said he realized this must be a shock to her, Dora, but not to worry. He intended to be scrupulously fair with the divorce settlement. He must have droned on for a good fifteen minutes while she numbly continued to chop celery and onions for the stew, as if by doing these homely things she could prevent him from tearing her world apart. Suddenly she turned toward him, interrupting. Her voice was low but as hard as the steel-bladed knife in her hand. "Let me see if I have this straight. You want to divorce me and marry Muriel, the waitress at the Wagon Wheel?" She gave a short laugh, more like a bark. "You are a fool, Ron. Now get out of here and let me finish making supper."

After she had browned the meat, then added vegetables and stock to the pot, she left the stew simmering on the stove and walked into the den. Ron was sitting in his recliner sipping his drink and staring off into space. She took a seat on the couch and began to speak to him, slowly and directly, not losing her temper. She pointed out that divorcing her would be impossible. She reminded him that everything they owned had come from her, and that his job at the bank barely covered the mortgage payment on the house. She had wondered out loud if his little slut knew the truth about his financial situation. Finally, she explained as if she were talking to a child that he would most likely lose his job if he foolishly went through with such a scheme. "Just imagine yourself squiring her to dinner at the club." She laughed lightly. "Really, Ron, you have had some silly ideas, but this is the most absurd. Think about it, and I'm sure you'll come to your senses by morning."

She had gone off to bed in the guest room and tossed through the night. Would he come to his senses? Men could be absolute fools sometimes. Well, if he didn't, she would have to find some way to stop him from ruining both their lives.

THE GOLF CART PATH hugged the woods past two tee boxes, then meandered alongside the fairways toward the clubhouse and pool area. Dora panted as her feet pounded the gravel track. Out of the corner of her eye, she saw the next-door neighbor's basset hound squeeze under the hedge and trot toward the track, wagging her backside in greeting. Still jogging in place, Dora bent down, picked up a pebble, and threw it at the dog, who gave her a reproachful look and retreated to her own yard.

She was unaware of the eyes glittering from the shadows behind one of the clapboard equipment sheds, or of the soft footsteps making prints in the dew as they followed her home at the end of her run.

SONNY SMART SLOWED his bicycle in front of the Crain house. He dismounted and carefully tossed the *Dallas Morning News,* then, shading his eyes with his hand, peered at a certain second-story window. He knew from past experience that this was Patty's bedroom. Once, he had been lucky enough to catch a glimpse of her tousled head as she looked down at the street. She had actually waved at him. Sonny was helplessly and hopelessly in love. He remounted his bike and pedaled slowly down the street, tossing newspapers into shrubbery and under parked cars as he went.

Jackson Crain often commented on the remarkable fact that his paper was the only one on the block that inevitably landed squarely in front of the door.

VANESSA LARGENT STARED morosely at the greasy dishwater in her kitchen sink, wishing it would disappear. It wouldn't, of course, and she suspected it was because of the coleslaw she'd emptied down the drain after supper last night. Who knew a few little slivers of cabbage could cause such a mess? Surely there had been only a few tablespoons left in the bowl. Oh, well, she thought, I'll just have to call the plumber. Steve won't have to be bothered. She'd pay Milt Piper out of her own money, money from the trust Gram had left. Lately, it seemed a good portion of that money was going toward hiding things from Steve, stupid things she'd done without thinking. Steve would be angry if he knew. He held old-fashioned ideas about living off his wife's money.

"Besides," he had said, "it would be unseemly for a pastor to live ostentatiously."

"But that's why Gram left me the money." Vanessa looked earnestly in his eyes. "She wanted me to have a nice life."

Gram, an actress, was not Vanessa's grandmother, she was her mother's older sister. She had loved Vanessa as her own, and Vanessa had returned her affection. Funny and brave and flamboyant, Gram would sweep into the little house where Vanessa lived with her parents and suddenly the place would fill with glamour and infinite possibility. When she died, Vanessa became heir to modest legacy that, prudently invested, had grown to a sizable sum of money.

Vanessa brushed a strand of hair out of her eyes and stood for a moment, trying to think where she'd left the plumber's number.

At thirty-two, Vanessa was a striking woman. Full shiny hair the color of a new copper penny formed a halo around her heart-shaped face with its tiny turned-up nose. Her eyes, greenish blue and expressive, gave away her every mood, sparkling with amusement when she was happy, dark and threatening when she was angry. And her temper matched her red hair. To please Steve, she tried to do everything possible to hide her good looks. It was not that he had ever actually suggested such a thing. It was the little remarks he had made. Like two summers ago when she had bought new sandals and painted her toenails scarlet to set them off. Steve had suggested that she wear closed shoes to the church picnic. And once, he had asked her to tone down her makeup—not abandon it completely. After all, these were modern times and they were Baptist, not Pentecostal. Just, maybe, wear a lighter shade of lipstick and not put on as much mascara. He thought the ladies of the congregation might feel more comfortable with her if she did. Vanessa thought they felt plenty comfortable already, always popping in unannounced and too quick with their unsolicited advice. But, because she loved Steve so much, she did her best to mold herself into his image of a proper clergyman's wife.

Vanessa opened the breadbox and retrieved a package of Salems from the middle of a loaf of white bread. She always hid her cigarettes in the white bread because she knew Steve would as soon break the seventh commandment as to eat white bread. She poured herself a cup of coffee and, taking a cigarette from the pack, lit it from the gas stove, then sank into a chair at the kitchen table.

As she smoked, Vanessa wondered how she and Steve had come to this place in their lives. Certainly she had never intended to be a minister's wife. Steve had been a Navy lieutenant when they'd met in Pensacola; she'd been nineteen and a commander's daughter. She smiled, remembering moonlight picnics on the beach followed by glorious sex in the sand. And later, in their first tiny apartment, candlelit dinners during which, tipsy from love and wine, they'd assured each other things would never change. Back then, they had shared the same hopes and dreams: a place in the country where they would grow their own food and have lots of kids and animals. There would be plenty of stars at night and red sunsets to watch as they held hands after supper. During the day, she would paint pictures, and he would write brilliant novels.

It had been the second year of their marriage when everything changed. Steve had flown to Washington for a one-day seminar. He would spend one night in a hotel, then fly back by noon the next day.

"I should be through with classes by six. I'll have dinner in my room, then call you. Sure you'll be okay?" Steve had raised an eyebrow and grinned.

"Of course, silly" she'd said, hugging him tightly, then shoving him toward the door. "Just hurry back, you hear?"

But Steve didn't call that night.

Vanessa was frantic by the time he got home the next morning but, because she loved him, was quiet while he told his story. He had chosen not to eat in the hotel, he said, and decided to walk to an Italian deli he'd seen on the corner down the block. On the way, he had passed a large brick church. She remembered how his eyes had sparkled when he got to that part.

"Van, there was this huge crowd of people waiting to get in; the line curled all the way around the building." Steve, sitting opposite her on the bed, took her hands in his. "And the people were smiling and talking to each other, Van, not minding that the line was long and the wind was cold. All kinds of people, black, white, parents, grandparents, teenagers, even little kids. Everyone seemed happy, like they shared some glorious secret!''

Steve's curiosity got the best of him, so he had blown off dinner and gone to the church service. His eyes glowed as he told her he had dedicated his life to serve the Lord that night. Would she come with him?

Vanessa ground out her cigarette and shook her auburn curls to clear away the memory. Where could that phone book be? she wondered, pawing through a pile of mail and magazines on the breakfast bar. Ah, here it was. Now, if she could just locate the phone. She found it under a pile of laundry on the breakfast table. Just as she started to dial, she glanced out the window at the roses climbing outside her door. Her eyes fell on one perfect rose, which must have opened during the night. Clinging to its petals, she saw three shimmering drops of dew. In an instant, Vanessa forgot all about the clogged drain. Grabbing her sketchpad and pastels, she slipped out the back door and was immediately lost to everything but the act of capturing the delicate perfection of that rose on paper.

She never heard the branches rustle behind the privet hedge.

FOUR

SHERIFF LEONARD J. GIBBS was a man of medium height, florid of face, and full in the belly. He was halfway through his second term as sheriff of Post Oak County. He had been a rancher most of his life except for a stint in the Air Force during Vietnam, when he had served as a military policeman. After Nam, he had come home and married his high school sweetheart. His marriage had been successful and deeply satisfying, his ranching career less so. Sheriff Gibbs was not cut out to live off the land. The vicissitudes of the weather drove him up the wall. One year drought, the next so much rain it was impossible to cut and bale hay. And the cows. How he hated cows! They were stupid creatures who stubbornly insisted on going in precisely the opposite direction from where you wanted them to be. He was just about at the end of his rope, what with the price of cattle on the hoof down to $1.49 a pound, when Sheriff Robinson had dropped dead from a stroke. He had run in the special election and won. He put his ranch on the market and quickly moved himself and his wife into the roomy apartment on the ground floor of the jail.

Today, he sat at his kitchen table drinking coffee.

He peered at the mug in his hand. His wife, whose hobby was ''crafting,'' as she called it, had painted something the sheriff decided must be bluebonnets on the side. Beneath the bluebonnets, he could see a tangle of squiggly lines he took to be letters.

''What's this you wrote on the side of this cup?'' He smiled at his wife, who was standing by the stove frying ham.

''Let's see,'' she said, forking a piece of ham onto a platter.

He held the cup aloft.

She came over to the table and took the mug out of his hand. ''That's not writing.'' She grinned. ''If you had one speck of the artistic temperament, you'd know that's a picture of some trees in the woods. Down there at the bottom, that's three little squirrels sittin' under the trees. And up in the sky, those blue things? Those are clouds. Here, let me get you some hot coffee. This stuff's colder than last night's dishwater.''

When she brought the coffee and set it on the table in front of him, he stretched out an arm and grabbed her around the waist. ''Clouds ain't blue; they're white—or maybe gray, sometimes.''

''They're my clouds, and I'll paint them any color I want to,'' she said, planting a kiss on his bald spot. ''It's called artistic license.''

''Well,'' he said, pulling her down on his lap, ''if you had to get a license for it, you'd never pass the test.''

She laughed. ''If you hate it so much, why'd you build me that nice worktable in the den so I could do my crafts and watch TV with you? Huh, Mr. Smarty Pants? And tell me how come you went all over town bragging about the hand-painted tie I made for your birthday.'' She slid off his lap. ''Now, do you want any of these beans, or just a ham sandwich?''

''Just a sandwich,'' he said. ''Judge Crain came by the office this morning. He says somebody's been hanging around the Rice mansion lately. Says whoever it is has got the old man and his wife good and spooked. He wants me to put Dooley on patrol there at night.''

His wife put a small plate containing a ham sandwich and a pickle in front of him. ''Are you going to?''

''Reckon I'll have to. Can't take any chances, although if you ask me, them two are just plain senile. You know they don't eat right on account of him being so close with money. I seen on TV where you can get that old-timer's disease from poor nutrition. My guess is they've starved out most of their brain cells. Still and all, Jackson seems to be taking the matter seriously, and he ain't nobody's fool.'' He finished his sandwich and wiped his mouth with a stenciled napkin. ''You got any iced tea, Norma Jean?''

''Just a minute. I hear the doorbell.''

She left the room and came back followed by Dooley Burns. The deputy dropped into a chair next to the sheriff. He took out a handkerchief and mopped his brow.

''You ain't gonna believe what I just seen out on

Hall's Mill Road.'' Dooley paused for emphasis. "I know I wouldn't, if I hadn't seen it with my very own eyes.''

RON HUGHES HAD ARRIVED home from the dentist and was sitting on his patio drinking carrot juice. He had had two wisdom teeth pulled and, because of the novocaine, he'd lost control of his mouth. Before he realized what was happening, he had a large orange stain on the front of his white golf shirt. He stole a glance at his wife, who was lounging beside him on a large black beach towel, her eyes hidden behind a pair of huge Jackie O sunglasses. Ron hoped against hope that they were closed so he could slip back into the house and change before she saw what he had done. With luck, he could hide the shirt in the back of the hamper and claim complete ignorance when she grilled him about it the next morning. He hoped she was sleeping. Typically, she hadn't moved or acknowledged his presence since he'd come outside to wait for his foursome to tee off. She hadn't spoken to him since last night when he had told her about Muriel. Maybe he was wrong to have done that—or maybe he could have done it differently, been more tactful. Still, how could you tell your wife you were in love with another woman and do it tactfully? Lord, he had no experience in these matters. In retrospect, he wished he had been less honest, just told her he needed space, or some equally meaningless bit of psychobabble. The more he thought about it, the more he wished he had done that. Then, at least, she would have been spared her pride. And perhaps he would have been spared the full force of her anger. That's been my problem, he thought, always second-guessing myself, never sure whether I've done the right thing. One thing is certain. She can hurt me, and she will. There's got to be a way out of this, and I'm going to find it.

Shaking his head, he eased his large frame out of his chair, thankful Dora had made him oil all the patio furniture on Saturday, and crept into the house. In the bedroom, he stashed the shirt and slipped into a clean blue one. Might as well stroll over to the clubhouse for a drink, he thought, rubbing his now-tingling lips. As he silently eased the heavy front door shut, he noticed the neighbor's basset hound ambling into the yard.

"Go home, Blossom!" he called.

At the sound of her name, Blossom wagged her tail and started toward him.

Ron clapped his hands. "Go home, I say!"

Blossom sat down and scratched her ear, looking sadly at him, then got up and trotted toward the Hugheses' back yard.

"MEATLOAF!" Jackson rubbed his hands together as he entered his sunny yellow kitchen. "My favorite."

Lutie Faye was poking pats of butter into a steaming bowl of mashed potatoes. "Tell that to the young'un." She waved her fork toward Patty. "She say she ain't eatin' nothin' but a mayonnaise sandwich for lunch."

Patty, wearing khaki shorts and a white T-shirt, was standing at the counter. She had just slapped a heaping tablespoonful of mayonnaise on a slice of white bread. "I love it." She licked the spoon. "Mmm, mayonnaise sandwiches and iced tea."

Jackson seated himself at the kitchen table. "Leave her alone, Lutie," he said. "When I was her age, I spent an entire summer eating nothing but cold hot dogs. Do we have any of those butter beans left?"

"Butter beans don't go with meatloaf. *Spinach* go with meatloaf." Lutie set a bowl of creamed spinach in front of him. "Now ya'll go on and eat. I got washing to do at home."

Patty joined him at the table. She held a sandwich in one hand and a glass of tea in the other.

"What are your plans for the afternoon?" Jackson asked.

"Swim at the club."

"Going alone?"

"Uh-uh. A bunch of us are riding our bikes out." Patty got up to retrieve the mayonnaise and bread from the counter.

"Good-looking guys out there?" Jackson had a twinkle in his eye.

"Oh, Daddy!"

"Well, I know Rick Barnes is lifeguarding this summer."

"He's ancient, Daddy. A sophomore!" Patty turned pink. "Anyway, it's a birthday party, sort of. For Sonny Smart."

Jackson helped himself to another slice of meatloaf. "Well, do you need a present?"

"I got him some comic books." Patty didn't really want to talk about it anymore. "Can I be excused?"

"Sure," Jackson said. "There's a present for you

on the hall table. It's from the Rices, thanking you for your quick thinking at the café.''

Patty squirmed out of her chair and made for the hall. In an instant, she was back with the package. She wrinkled her nose. "Eee-yew," she said, "this paper is positively *antediluvian!*"

Jackson hid a grin. "Open it, and let's see what they gave you."

Patty ripped open the package and withdrew an obviously secondhand white blouse. She held it up with two fingers. "Gross," she said.

The blouse, cotton with tiny tucks running up the front, had a ruffled collar and pearl buttons. Although it had been carefully washed and ironed, he could see at the neckline an unmistakable tea stain. She gave it a shake, then dropped it on the floor on top of the paper.

"Well, it's the thought that counts," Jackson said. He picked up the blouse and placed it back in the box. "Maybe you can give it to the church rummage sale."

"You better not do that," Lutie broke in. "Them old folks probably gonna be all over that sale tryin' to pick up bargains."

Jackson grinned and returned his attention to Lutie's delicious lunch.

FIVE

BACK IN HIS OFFICE, the sheriff faced Dooley across his desk. "Well, spit it out. What did you see?"

Dooley hooked his long body around a captain's chair in front of the sheriff's desk and removed his straw Stetson, placing it carefully on the corner of the desk. Then with both hands he tried to smooth the hat marks from his thinning, blondish hair. Next he drew a red pack of Marlboros out of his shirt pocket and lit one with a kitchen match, watching the sheriff out of the corner of his eye, trying to gauge how long it would take him to explode.

"Goddamit, boy! Open your mouth and talk."

Dooley took a long and satisfying pull from his cigarette, then began to speak. "Wellsir, it happened like thisaway, don'tcha know. I was patrolling 557 out near the lake when I picked up old L. C. Warrick on my scanner. He was talking on his CB radio." Dooley's voice got even more high-pitched than usual as he warmed to his story. "Hell, old L.C. was talking so fast, I couldn't hardly tell what he was saying, so I says, 'Slow down, L.C., I can't make nothing out of that gibberish.' Wellsir, he commences talking a little bit slower, and what he said was, somebody had come on his place and killed four of his breed goats, one being that big Boer billy he just got. Told me he paid upwards of four thousand for that thing.''

The sheriff got up and poured himself another cup of coffee, then filled Dooley's cup. "Go on," he said.

"Well, I seen that goat when he was alive. He was big as a donkey and smelled a sight worse. Anyway, I arrived on the scene and secured the area.''

"Secured the area?''

"Well, a goodly crowd of neighbors had come over to gawk, don'tcha know. I told them to stand back.''

"Hmm." The sheriff nodded. "Go on.''

"Sheriff, it was awful. Them sumbitches had cut the poor critter's head off and stuck it up on a fence post. The rest of the carcass was laying on the ground next to it.''

"Did you turn up any evidence? Footprints? Tire tracks?''

"Hell, no. Them nosy neighbors had stomped all over any evidence that might have been there.'' Dooley paused and scratched his head. "There was one thing, though.''

"What?''

"If I hadn't seen it, I wouldn't of believed it.''

"Well, what?''

"They'd gone and cut that poor animal's nuts out! They was laying right there in the grass.'' Dooley looked around and lowered his voice. "Sheriff, them things were big as cantaloupes!''

THE KNITTER'S NOOK sat on Main Street between the post office and Ye Olden Treasures Antique Shoppe. The building had been a hardware store back in the days when horse collars, whiffletrees, churns, and anvils were basic necessities of life. Sometime in the thirties, the building had been divided in half lengthwise and had housed a barbershop on one side and a small lunchroom on the other. When cousins Esther and Jane Archer purchased the property, it had stood empty for ten years. As many years of grease and grime covered the walls and the small show window at the front. A narrow shelf designed to display merchandise stood behind the window. The sisters cleaned for a month, carting off ten pickup loads of debris from the concrete floors. Then they set out to give the place a good cleaning. When they had finished, the floors were covered with sisal mats and the windows, draped in lace, sparkled. The tiny shelf displayed dolls dressed in hand-sewn outfits, afghans, dainty crocheted doilies, and colorful yarns and trims for every imaginable application. Inside, bins and shelves spilled over with more merchandise. The place was neat and cozy and a natural gathering place for the ladies of Post Oak. Here, the latest news was delivered, dissected, sorted, and hurled back onto the street with lightning speed.

Today, Annabeth Jones occupied an easy chair near the window, working on needlepoint cushions for the chancel rail at First Methodist, while Mae Applewaite, in an identical chair across the room, struggled with the intricacies of the cable stitch as she knitted a sweater for her grandson in Maine. Esther, small and birdlike, busied herself with the teapot, while Jane, who tipped the scales at 290 and favored men's clothing, sorted charge slips with huge, hairy hands.

"Personally, I can't understand all the excitement about arugula." Mae put down her knitting because she couldn't concentrate on that and talk at the same time. "To me, it tastes like raw turnip greens, but you can't pick up a copy of *Southern Living* anymore without seeing a recipe for some salad made with the stuff."

"I know," said Annabeth. "It's the same with *pesto*. My lord, you'd think we all came from Sicily or something. Give me a good slab of iceberg with homemade thousand island any old day."

"Or tomato aspic with mayonnaise on top," boomed Jane from the counter.

Esther entered carrying a large tea tray. "Speaking of tomato aspic," she said, "Hazelle Perkins served that at our last bridge luncheon. It was canned!"

"Not Hazelle!" Mae was shocked. "She prides herself on making everything from scratch."

"Not this time," Esther said. "I saw the cans with my own two eyes—right there in her kitchen trash. Well, I couldn't help seeing it. I had to get a drink of water so I could take my blood pressure pill, didn't I? How did I know she'd leave those cans right there on top for the world and everybody to see?"

Jane remembered what a good customer Hazelle was. "Now, be nice, cousin," she said.

"I'll have to admit, it was probably better than what she could make from scratch." Esther refused to be nice. "Who wants lemon?"

"I'll take milk," said Annabeth. "Oh, look! There comes Myrtice Rice down the sidewalk. Lord, she looks like she can hardly navigate."

"My soul, looks like she's coming here." Mae craned her neck toward the window.

Jane came over and stood beside Mae. "Probably wants one spool of thread. That's all the poor thing ever buys—and that so she can mend her pitiful old clothes. Shh, here she comes." Jane scurried back to her position behind the counter.

The bell over the door tinkled as Myrtice Rice entered the shop.

"Come on in, Mrs. Rice," Jane called. "Have a seat and let Esther pour you a cup of tea. My, it's a scorcher today, isn't it?"

Mrs. Rice perched on a straight chair next to the wall. "Thank you, dear," she said. "A cup of tea would be just lovely."

"I heard you had a little spell at the café Sunday evening," Mae said. "Nothing serious, I hope."

"Oh, no." Mrs. Rice smoothed her beautiful white hair. "It was nothing. Silly me, I choked on a piece of pie. I have been having some difficulty swallowing lately. I can't imagine why."

"Nerves," Esther said. "Either that or you might have a hiatal hernia. My mother had that. She couldn't eat anything but a little tomato soup and vanilla ice cream for the last year of her life."

"Oh, dear." Mrs. Rice accepted the tea Esther handed her.

"Have you seen the doctor?" Annabeth asked.

"No, I—"

"Never mind, it's probably just nerves." Mae knew the poor woman's husband would never allow her to see a doctor.

Myrtice Rice finished her tea and set the cup on the counter.

"Well, the main thing is, you're okay now," Jane said heartily. "What can I get for you?"

"Just a spool of white mercerized cotton, small." Mrs. Rice opened her mouth to say more, then snapped it shut.

Jane selected the thread from the spool rack and put it in a small paper bag. "Put this on your bill?"

"No, I—I'll pay cash." She dug into her purse and pulled out two quarters. "Will this cover it?"

"With change back," Jane said. "Now, you take care of yourself. Don't go letting your nerves get the best of you."

Mrs. Rice took the bag and change and started for the door. With her hand on the knob, she turned to face the others.

"I am *not* nervous." Her voice quavered. "What would I have to be nervous about? Anyway, it's nobody's business if I am a little edgy these days. Nobody's business at all!"

With that, she walked out, slamming the door behind her.

"Well, I swan!" Annabeth said.

"What do you think of that?" said Mae.

"She's nervous, all right." Jane waved her ballpoint at them.

"I wonder why," mused Esther.

SIX

BLOSSOM SQUEEZED under the fence and trotted across the Hugheses' front lawn. Her senses told her something—something of uncommon interest—might be in the offing. Nose to the ground, she headed toward the house. When she reached the viburnum hedge, she veered to the left and proceeded around the corner of the house, pausing to examine something on the ground. Nothing of interest here, only the calling card of the schnauzer from across the street. She next visited the Japanese maple in the side yard and was disappointed to find only the scent of squirrels. Experience had taught Blossom not to waste energy on squirrels. Annoying creatures, they ignored her attempts at conversation, instead stuffed their cheeks full of nuts, and scurried up the trees to chatter peevishly down at her. As if she were the least bit interested in stealing their nuts! And as for chasing them, well, she had better things to do. Blossom paused to scratch herself, then, crossing the still-fresh trail of a field mouse, made her way around back.

The flagstone patio felt hot to her pads, but something irresistible propelled her forward. Her nose stopped at a still form lying on a beach towel. She touched the thing with her paw. It did not move. With her nose, she rooted underneath the object. The scent was faint but unmistakable. Edging her body next to it, she rubbed her back against it from end to end. Large black sunglasses fell to the ground with a clatter. Blossom jumped and retreated to the edge of the patio. She sat for a moment, watching, then cautiously returned for a look. Blind eyes stared up at the branches of a willow tree. A crow cawed loudly as Blossom nudged the object with her nose, enjoying the scent. She gave a tentative scratch with one stubby paw. When there was no response, she climbed on top of the thing and stared into its sightless eyes. Finally, satisfied it was safe, Blossom rolled over. Paws in the air, she arched her back. Heaven! Digging her head into the lifeless flesh, she squirmed happily, wriggling like a snake until, exhausted, she scrambled down and trotted happily home, thinking about a large drink of water and a nap under the pomegranate tree before suppertime.

SEVEN

IT WAS A GORGEOUS DAY, cloudless with just a hint of fall. Football weather, everybody said. The air in the Wagon Wheel was much the same at any time of year. Rip had never established a nonsmoking area, so the thin mist of cigarette smoke that hung in the air mingled with the scent of coffee and the disinfectant Muriel had used to mop the kitchen earlier. To the afternoon coffee crowd, it was not the least bit unpleasant.

"Did you see it?" Rip came up to the booth where Jackson and newspaper editor Horace Kinkaid, a plump little bantam rooster of a man with red hair, were having afternoon coffee.

"See what?" Jackson tasted his coffee and made a face. It was cold.

Rip squeezed into the booth beside Horace. "Well, hell, the goddam sign out front that the goddam Main Street Committee made me put up. It's a wonder you didn't bump your head on it when you walked in here. It's a cinch somebody's gonna do that very thing, and I'll get sued sure as shit stinks."

Jackson squirmed around in his seat to look outside. "I don't see it."

"See what?" Brother Steve Largent had just

pushed open the door and was approaching their table.

"It's the god—the dadgummed Main Street Committee. They've gone and—"

Horace interrupted. "Go get the preacher his decaf. We'll tell him all about it."

"I'll have a piece of that apple pie, too," the reverend called after Rip. "Vanessa burned the soup again at lunch. I don't even know how a person could burn *soup!* Now, what's Rip got his shorts in a knot about?" He addressed Jackson.

"I reckon you ought to let Rip tell you," Horace butted in. "He needs to blow off a little of that head of steam he's built up."

The preacher shrugged and waited for Rip to come back with his pie and coffee. "Where's Muriel?" he asked, cutting into his pie.

"In the back," Rip said. "She's taken one of them cleaning binges she gets ever once in a while. Did you see it?"

"See what?" Brother Largent chewed his pie with relish.

Horace looked at Jackson and rolled his eyes.

"The goldurned new sign." Rip's finger shook as he pointed toward the window. "Hell, it's hanging over the sidewalk. Looks like something you'd find at one of them gift shops. Those committee ladies and that new woman they sent up here out of Austin sent me a certified letter saying my neon sign wasn't in keeping with the *ambience* of a Main Street City, whatever the hell that is. Next thing you know, they'll be makin' me hang up some goddam lace curtains in the goddam window.'' Rip forgot to clean up his language for the preacher. ''Said I had to take my other sign down—it was the law. That right, Jackson?'' The grubby sailor hat Rip wore when he cooked shook with indignation.

''I doubt it.'' Jackson grinned. ''Still, you being a civic-minded citizen and all—''

Suddenly Rip noticed Jackson hadn't touched his coffee. ''What's wrong with that?'' He pointed to Jackson's cup.

''It's cold.''

Rip picked up Jackson's mug, then looked at Horace. ''How 'bout yours?''

''I like it that way.'' Horace took a sip to prove it.

Rip went behind the bar and poured a fresh cup for Jackson. When he came back to the table, Horace had an idea. ''How about I take your picture for the paper—standing next to your brand-new sign?''

Rip brightened. ''For the paper?''

''Sure.'' Horace winked at Jackson. ''It'll look great in that quarter-page ad you're going to buy.''

''Ad? I ain't takin' no ad. Why would I want to take out a ad, for crissake? I got the only café in town, don't I?''

''Well, maybe we could put in a little human interest story.'' Horace drained his coffee cup. ''You're sure as hell interesting—I'm not too sure about the human part, though.''

''Let's get going, then,'' Rip said, getting to his feet. ''I ain't got all day to mess around, like some folks I know.''

Jackson finished his coffee and followed the pair out to the sidewalk. The preacher followed.

The sign, oval in shape and made of varnished wood, had letters carved in script spelling out the name of the café. Jackson had to agree that Rip's old neon beer sign was more in keeping with the nature of the establishment.

"Stand over there." Horace indicated a spot next to the sign. "Now smile, dammit. That is, if you're capable."

Rip made an expression that could have been a smile or a wince. "Hurry up and take the thing. I can't hold this here smile all day."

"Okay, chin up, now. Here goes—well, dadgummit, Sheriff, now you've gone and spoiled the shot!"

The sheriff had pulled into a parking space in front of the café and was hurrying toward Jackson.

"You'd better come with me, Judge," he said. "Something awful bad has happened."

"Right." Jackson followed him to the car.

Brother Steve followed. "Do you need me, Sheriff?"

The sheriff shook his head. "Not now, maybe later, Preacher."

Jackson slid into the front seat of the brown Ford with the county logo on the side and slammed the door as Sheriff Gibbs put the car in gear and guided it onto Main Street. He waited silently for the sheriff to speak, noting that they were heading toward the country club.

"Judge, I don't hardly know how to tell you this…"

"What? My God, it's not Patty?" Jackson remembered she'd gone swimming at the club. "Speak up, man!"

"Lord, no!" The sheriff could have kicked himself for scaring the judge. "It's that sister-in-law of yours."

"Dora? What happened?"

The sheriff's face was grim. "She's dead. Murdered."

Jackson looked out the window at the telephone poles flashing by, his heart pounding. Thank God it wasn't Patty. He unwrapped a Don Diego, rolled down the car window, and lit the cigar. The sheriff glanced his way, then continued.

"Ron Hughes found her. Came in off the golf course and there she was, laying on the patio. He said he knew right away something was wrong because she hadn't moved since he'd left to play golf."

"How long was that? About three hours?"

"Maybe more'n that. See, Ron, he'd gone to the dentist, and when he came home, she was taking a sunbath—or that's what he thought at the time." The sheriff turned onto Country Club Drive. "He says he went out and sat with her on the patio for a little while, but she didn't say nothing. Ron says that's not unusual. Seems they didn't get along all that good."

Jackson nodded. "Where's Ron now?"

"He's back at the house. Dooley called the paramedics, and I jumped in the car to come get you." He turned the car into the Hugheses' driveway. "Look's like they just got here."

Jackson got out of the car and walked up to the

ambulance just as two attendants, a man and a woman, were removing a stretcher from the rear of the vehicle.

"Have you examined her yet?"

The woman turned to face him, and he saw it was Amy Tubbs. She was tall and black, her long hair braided and held back by a rubber band. "Oh, Judge Crain, it's you. Yes, sir. I'm afraid she's dead."

"How?"

"Well, Judge…" The woman was looking at a point somewhere beyond his left shoulder. "It looks like she was strangled…"

"Strangled?"

"…and that's not all. Somebody hit her on the head—from behind. Her skull was crushed." She swallowed hard. "I've been doing this kind of work for four years now, and I'm telling you the truth, I've never seen anything like this." She finally met his eyes. "Judge, after they did it to her, whoever it was, well, then they just laid her out on a towel to make it look like she was sunbathing. It's sick!"

The sheriff looked at the stretcher. "And you were going to move her?"

"Well, yes. Mr. Hughes told us to. And your deputy said it was okay."

"Load that thing up and get it out of here," the sheriff barked. "We'll have her moved when we get through with our investigation. I shouldn't have left," he said to Jackson as they rounded the corner of the house. "That Dooley don't have the sense God promised a… Godamighty! Get that damn dog out of here!"

Dooley, who had been sitting in a lawn chair, grabbed Blossom by the collar and pulled her over to the garden shed. He shoved her in and weighed the door shut with a rock.

Jackson stood looking down at what had been his sister-in-law. The body had been turned on its side, and he could see a gaping hole in the back of the head. A triangle of skin was laid back, revealing a quarter-inch crack in the skull. The hair was flattened around the wound and matted with blood. The skin of her back was bare and livid where the blood had pooled. He fought back nausea as he glanced around at the patio area.

"She had to have been moved here," he said softly. "Sheriff, why don't you and Dooley examine the premises. I'll go in and talk to Ron."

"Right." The sheriff sprung into action. "Dooley, go out to the car and get your fingerprint kit—and bring that can of luminol. I want this whole area dusted and sprayed—inside and out. Judge, why don't you put in a call to Shelby Grayson. He's gonna want to know about this."

Jackson entered the house by the kitchen door and stopped to telephone the district attorney. He spoke briefly into the phone before heading toward the bedroom, where he found Ron sitting on the edge of the bed staring at a sock in his hand as if he'd never seen it before.

EIGHT

MYRTICE RICE HUMMED as she swept the cavernous kitchen in the brown brick mansion she shared with her husband. Her best times were after lunch when Ray went down for his nap, and she was alone with her thoughts, which increasingly seemed to dwell in the past. She glanced about the bleak room, with its crumbling tiles and faded wallpaper, remembering how it once was. Warm and welcoming, with sunlight streaming through the tall windows, the kitchen had been the hub of the household. Afternoons, the air was fragrant with the scent of cookies baking or a ham sizzling in the oven for the night's dinner. And at three, the screen door would slam and the room would be full of hungry boys eager to fill their hands with cookies before going off to their next important project, whether it be building a treehouse in the ancient elm tree or constructing a model airplane in the attic playroom. The door of the huge Westinghouse refrigerator had always sported colorful magnets holding family snapshots or the most recent drawings of airplanes, horses, and cars Raymond created by the score. Then her thoughts drifted farther afield. She smiled, remembering a time when she was young and the most popular girl in town. Suitors had swarmed around her door—or that's how it seemed now, looking back. Then Ray Rice came home from college, ready to go into his father's business and make his fortune. She smiled when she remembered what a dashing figure he'd made in his porkpie hats and bell-bottom trousers. He'd been a big spender, too, showering her with gifts and taking her for banana splits at the ice-cream parlor. It was only later he'd changed. After the Depression devastated the country, cotton prices had plummeted. His father broke under the strain and put a gun to his head. Ray had become a man possessed, determined to recover his father's lost fortune. Then the child, Raymond, Jr., had come. No, she wouldn't think about Raymond, Jr.

She put away the broom and opened the ancient refrigerator. Inside, she saw a quart of buttermilk, half a pan of cornbread, and a small saucer on which rested a sliver of bacon rind and a tablespoonful of leftover scrambled eggs. Picking up the saucer, she went to the back door and pushed open the screen.

"Here, kitty-kitty-kitty." She spoke softly, so as not to wake Raymond. She looked toward the ramshackle grape arbor, where the cat usually napped in the shade. "Come get your dinner, baby kitty. Come on, now."

She set the saucer down on the bottom step and turned to go back in the house, then paused. Where could that cat be? She turned again and took a few steps across the yard. "Kitty?"

Just then, she heard a voice from inside the house. "Myrtice? I believe I'll have a glass of buttermilk now, if you please."

She hurried back up the steps and opened the screen door, glancing worriedly toward the grape arbor.

THE MAIN STREET CITY offices were located in a yellow bungalow on Birch Street just a half block from the courthouse. The house, one of many of its kind in the town, was built in 1921 from a kit ordered from a catalog. A wooden front porch, held up by four brick columns, extended the width of the house, with concrete steps leading up to it. An old-fashioned front door with sidelights stood directly in front of the steps. Two rooms fronted the house on either side of a center hall. One room was used as a reception room, while the other served as the private office of the director. The rooms in the rear were used for storage. Two window air-conditioning units, like ears, jutted out on either side of the building.

Mandy de Alejandro sat at her desk, going over the latest grant proposals for refurbishing the city park and wondering what in the world she was doing here. When this job had become available, she had been working in the Austin offices as executive secretary to the chairman of the commission. She had jumped at the chance, determined to get away from the capital city, which was bursting at its seams with newcomers, mostly technical workers who had moved to town in the wake of the rapidly growing dot.com industry. Now Austin threatened to outpace the Silicon Valley in size and scope. Traffic had become unbearable and shopping a chore. When the rent on her one-bedroom apartment had skyrocketed to $1,100 a month in less than a year, she had vowed to leave.

And she had to admit Brad had played a part. After a year, she still found herself blushing when she thought of him. The relationship was passionate at first, and she had been carried away by emotions she never dreamed she was capable of. He was from California, new in town, a product of the tech revolution. They met on the hike-and-bike trail that surrounded Town Lake. Looking back, it was trite, really. They had each been walking their dogs, hers a Highland terrier and his a huge black Lab. As they passed each other on the trail, his Lab, Smoky, suddenly whirled around and followed her dog, Pocita, sniffing eagerly and wagging his huge tail. They had stopped to chat while the dogs got acquainted and ended up having coffee at Starbucks. Things moved too fast, she now thought; their mutual attraction was palpable, and when he asked her out that very night for dinner she had ended up in his bed. Now she felt embarrassed by it all. What had gotten into her? She had never been easy before. Barely six months passed before he grew tired of her and was off in search of new thrills, leaving Mandy unsure of herself and aching with the loss and confusion of it all. Now she was left wondering if she would ever find such a love again. Did she even want to? Surely there must be something better, she told herself, something easy and comfortable as well as sensual, a love that engaged the mind and heart as well as the body. She shook her head to erase the thoughts. She had a new life and a new home, and certainly her hands were full with this challenging new job.

Challenging though it was, in the short months she'd been in Post Oak, she had learned that a small town could offer its own brand of problems. She was finding herself bombarded from every side by opposing agendas. The Kiwanis Club wanted to refurbish the Little League park, while the Chamber of Commerce was pushing for an industrial park. The Ladies' Garden Club wanted new brick sidewalks with flower boxes all along Main Street.

She glanced at the wall clock. Almost three—time for her appointment with the mayor and the city council. Sliding open the desk drawer, she pulled out a small mirror and scrutinized her face. No repairs needed, she thought, examining her too-pug nose and creamy skin. Green eyes lined with a fringe of dark lashes gazed back at her. She hastily applied lipstick and ran a comb through her thick black curls, then, picking up her purse, left the office, locking the door behind her.

NINE

BROTHER STEVE OPENED the front door of the parsonage and was enveloped by the rich smell of frying chicken. He removed his suit coat, hung it on a peg on the hall tree, and made straight for the kitchen, where he found Van, elbow-deep in flour, rolling out a piecrust on the counter. A bowl of sliced apples, redolent with cinnamon and sugar, sat nearby. He lifted his wife's fragrant hair and kissed her behind the left ear. "Company coming?"

"Only us. We're having a picnic tonight—in our own backyard." She lowered her voice. "Don't tell a soul, but I picked up a bottle of Chablis at the grocery today. We're going to be naughty."

When she turned to wrap her arms around his neck, she did look like a naughty child. He wiped a smudge of flour off her nose with one finger and kissed her lips, savoring the taste of her. When they finally drew apart, he lifted the lid from the skillet and inhaled the aroma of the chicken. Bother his diet. Bother the deacons. Tonight, they'd remember Pensacola and be kids again.

"Great, honey," he said, "just let me go upstairs and change."

When he came back down, the pie was bubbling

in the oven, the chicken was piled on a platter, and she had poured two glasses of chilled wine.

"Come and sit with me." She patted the couch beside her.

He sank gratefully onto the couch and sampled the wine, savoring its tart sweetness. For just a moment, he felt a pang of guilt, but it was gone in an instant because now she was nibbling his neck, then his ear, and the minister was soon carried away in the fire of passion she could always ignite.

They made love right there on the couch, then lay entwined in each other's arms until the phone rang shrilly.

"Oh, no. My pie!"

Steve dived for the phone while Vanessa headed for the stove. She grabbed a mitt and opened the oven door.

"Good. It was just the juice running over…Steve, what is it?"

"I'll be right over," he said into the telephone. "Give me fifteen minutes." He put down the phone. "That was Jackson Crain. Dora Hughes was murdered. I have to go. Ron needs me."

ACROSS THE STREET, hidden by low-hanging branches, a man watched the preacher get into his car and drive off. His orders were to maintain constant surveillance on this house. It and its inhabitants were important aspects of his overall mission. He took a small cellular phone out of his inside pocket and spoke briefly into it, noting as he spoke that the downstairs lights were going out. He maintained his post until the light in the upstairs bedroom was turned on. Then he turned and disappeared into the shadows.

THE NEXT MORNING, Jackson stopped in at the Wagon Wheel for breakfast before going to the office.

"Jackson, you oughta get you some new clothes. Them things look like you got them out of the Goodwill box."

"Thanks." Jackson beamed up at Muriel. "Now, could you please get me some fresh coffee? This stuff tastes like antifreeze."

"Well, hell." Horace Kincaid slid into the booth opposite Jackson. "I left home to get away from yow-yowing, and now I have to hear it from the two of you."

Muriel ignored Horace. "All I'm saying is that there's a nice-looking young lady just moved to town, and she's not going to give you a second look."

"I'll have the sunrise special." Horace always got up starving. "Over easy."

"Who says I'm looking?" Jackson asked.

Muriel picked up Jackson's coffee mug and turned to go. "Just don't say I didn't warn you."

"Hey!" Horace said.

"I heard you," Muriel said over her shoulder. "Sunrise special. Over easy."

Horace grinned, then turned to Jackson. "Sorry to hear about Dora."

"Yeah, thanks."

"How's Patty taking it?"

"Okay, I guess. She was on the phone with her

friends all evening. I hate to admit it, but I think she's stimulated by the whole thing.''

"Well, that's kids for you. They don't understand death. Hell, they see it on TV all the time. Desensitizes them. When's the funeral?''

Jackson was studying the menu. "Don't know yet.'' He turned to Muriel, who had returned with fresh coffee. "Bring me the southwestern omelet with whole wheat toast.''

Muriel wrote down Jackson's order, then leaned over the table. "Did ya'll hear anything about them putting in one of them nuclear plants out east of town? A feller was in here this morning early. He was saying they've been surveying out on the old Mitcham place over west of the creek. He says, you watch and see, half the people in town will be coming down with cancer, not to mention two-headed calves and no tellin' what all else.''

"I heard something about it.'' Horace stirred sugar into his coffee. "But I couldn't get any hard facts. I suspect it's nothing but a rumor somebody's put out.''

"Maybe so.'' Muriel turned and went back behind the counter.

Horace watched her go. "Mighty good-looking gal. Shame that ex of hers is so sorry.''

"Mmm.''

"You represent her, don't you?''

"I got her divorce for her, if that's what you mean.'' Jackson disliked being questioned about clients, and Horace, ever the news hound, never failed to push for information.

Horace glanced at the bar, then leaned in closer.

"Well, don't say I said it, but the rumor's going around that she and your wife's brother-in-law have been having a little fling."

"Ah, here's our food." Jackson was relieved not to have to comment on Horace's last remark. He nodded to Muriel as she set their plates down, then sliced into the steaming omelet filled with picante sauce and cheese.

"HEY, JACKSON." Edna shoved a plate of cookies across her desk as he entered the office. "I sure was sorry to hear about Dora. Not that I ever had much use for her. She was just naturally a stuck-up bitch—but I wouldn't have wanted to see her dead. Not like that. You want some of these gingersnaps with your coffee? I made them just this morning."

"No, thanks." Jackson headed for his door. "Has Shelby Grayson called?"

"Only about forty times. He wants me to call him the minute you get here. Says he'll be right over. Shall I call him now?"

"I'll do it," Jackson said.

Five minutes later, the district attorney was seated in Jackson's office. Shelby Grayson was a compact man, about fifty, impeccably dressed in a black pin-striped suit.

"I've arranged for the sheriff to meet us here." He crossed his legs, carefully arranging the pleat in his trousers. "Sorry to hear about Dora."

"Thanks."

"How's Ron?"

"Pretty broken up about it."

"Oh? I heard they weren't getting along." The district attorney got down to business.

"Maybe. Did you bring a copy of his statement?"

Grayson opened his briefcase and passed the typewritten statement across the desk to Jackson. "Take your time reading it. I'll just ask Edna to give me a cup of coffee."

The statement was simple. Ron had come home from the dentist's and sat for a time with Dora on the patio. They had not spoken, but Ron was sure she was alive at the time. He had left at one-thirty for his round of golf and could prove his whereabouts from that time until four, when he returned home. When he found her still lying in the same position on the patio, he became alarmed and bent over to speak to her. When she did not respond, he touched her. It was then that he discovered she was dead. He had called emergency services at four-twenty.

Jackson put down the paper and glanced up at Grayson, who had returned with a mug of coffee and a plate of cookies. "What do we know about the time of death?"

"Ross Marshall puts it at between noon and three-thirty." Grayson referred to the town's only physician. "There was very little lividity, and no rigor. The body was still warm, but it would be, since she'd been lying in the sun all afternoon." Grayson picked up a cookie, looked at it, and put it back down on the plate. "The ME from San Antone will have to give us a full report. I've had the body sent down there, and I've told Ron he can't have a funeral until sometime next week. Oh, hello, Sheriff. Come on in."

The sheriff took the other leather chair opposite Jackson's desk.

"What about physical evidence?" Jackson asked.

"We found the murder weapon," Sheriff Gibbs said. "It was a rock about the size of a bowling ball. Whoever hit her with it chunked it out in the rough around the seventh green. We found bits of hair and blood still sticking to it. As for what she was strangled with, I don't know. By the look of the marks on her neck, I'd say it was somebody's bare hands."

"Where was all the blood?" Jackson folded his hands and leaned toward the sheriff. "From the size of that head wound, she must have bled a lot."

"Well, the towel was soaked with it—and the concrete under her. See, the thing is, that towel was black, so it didn't show all that much. Oh, yeah, and she had one of those foam rubber egg crate pads underneath the towel. All that's going to the ME's office along with the body."

"Which might explain why Ron didn't realize she was dead," Jackson said. "What else?"

"We found quite a bit of blood on the cart path behind the house. That says to me that either she was moved or the killer left it behind. Of course, we'll have to have it analyzed, too."

"I'll want to come by the jail and take a look at that rock," Jackson said. "Anything else?"

Grayson stood up. "That's about it, Jackson. You'd better find Ron a good criminal defense lawyer."

"I'll get him a lawyer," Jackson said. "He hasn't been indicted yet." He stood. "Now, if there's nothing else..."

"There is one other thing, Judge," Sheriff Gibbs said. "I know that woman was so persnickety, she wouldn't own a dog on a bet."

"That's true. Dora hated dogs."

"Wellsir, that's what's so strange. You would have thought she'd been holding one on her lap. She had dog hairs all over her."

TEN

IT WAS DARK before Jackson pulled his car into the driveway in back of the house. His feet crunched on the gravel pathway as he made his way to the rear door. A lone light from the kitchen etching a pattern on the grass told him Patty wasn't home yet. Once inside the house, he dropped his briefcase on the back hall table and entered the warm kitchen. Lutie Fay had left one of her terse notes: *Plate in the fridge. Chicken and rice. Heat in the microwave. Patty at band practice.* He shrugged out of his suit jacket and hung it over the back of a chair, then took down a glass and filled it with ice cubes, after which he opened the cabinet where he kept his liquor and withdrew a bottle of scotch. Then, drink in hand, he went into his study and sank gratefully into his worn leather armchair, realizing suddenly that he was bone-weary. He lit a Don Diego and watched the blue smoke curl upward, remembering the times he had seen his father sitting in this same old leather chair, a glass of scotch on the marble-topped table and a cigar near at hand. But I'm not my father, he thought. Old Judge Crain had been a lawyer of the old school, steeped in the majesty of the law and bound by the long-dead ethics of the profession. Jackson had never shared his father's ardent dedication. Once, he thought he wanted to be a police officer. His father had looked at Jackson as if he had announced that he wanted to run off and be a circus clown.

"You want to be a cop?" He set his drink down and looked levelly at his son.

"Yes, sir."

Jackson blushed, wishing he had kept his mouth shut. It had always been assumed that he would go to law school and follow in his father's footsteps.

"Dad, this doesn't mean I won't go to law school. I could use that in law enforcement, couldn't I? I want to work on a big-city police force, maybe be chief someday." He sat on the edge of the sofa and looked earnestly at his father, hoping for some glimmer of understanding. "It's just, well, crime…I don't know. It fascinates me. Always has."

"You think it's like those cop shows on television."

"No, sir. I don't, really. I'm not that stupid, Dad."

"Well, son, you're only sixteen. As long as you say you'll go to law school, we can decide on your future at a later date." The judge picked up his newspaper, indicating that the matter was settled.

But Jackson never forgot. His passion for police work did not diminish and, until his third year at the university, he fully intended to move toward that goal. Then his father had his first heart attack. After that, the once-powerful man seemed to shrink before Jackson's eyes until, by the time Jackson passed his bar exams, it seemed impossible not to come back home. Otherwise, the practice his father had worked so hard to preserve would disappear and the judge would die a brokenhearted man. Jackson and Gretchen moved into a little house on Cypress Street, resisting his mother's urgings to move into the big house, and allowed his name to be added to the shingle in front of his father's office. Within five years, old Judge Crain was dead, and a year later, his mother followed. But by this time, Patty had come along and Jackson had forgotten all about his early interest in police work.

Jackson sighed, then turned his thoughts to Dora's murder. He wished he could muster up a little sadness over her death. Anger? Yes, he felt that, and revulsion for the cold brutality of it all, but not sorrow. Jackson didn't dwell on it. He doubted if very many people in town would grieve for Dora. Despite all her good works, she was standoffish and loud and a terrible snob. Still, for all her faults, she hadn't deserved to die like that. Did Ron do it? God knows she'd made his life miserable enough. He couldn't count the times she had belittled him in public, reminding people that she was the one in the family with the money—and the brains. He thought about his conversation with Ron earlier that day.

Jackson had gone out to the house to invite Ron to spend a few days with him and Patty. When he had pushed open the kitchen door, he'd found Ron standing in the kitchen, a dishtowel in one hand. A few soiled glasses and a plate or two lay beside the sink. Ron Hughes was handsome in an all-American sort of way. Blond of hair and tanned from his daily rounds of golf, he stood over six feet, with broad shoulders and well-muscled arms. He had played football both in high school and college and still walked with the rolling gait of an athlete. It was only in the twitch of his mouth and the pale darting eyes that his intrinsic weakness revealed itself. Odd to see such a powerful man looking so helpless, Jackson thought.

"I thought I ought to wash these." He waved the dishtowel at Jackson. "You know how Dora was. But I don't know how to…" He looked down at the dishwasher.

Jackson pressed the lever to open the machine and dropped the dishes in. "Now," he said, "go into the den and sit down. I'm going to make us a drink, then we can discuss what needs to be done."

Soon they were both holding double scotches and were settled into Dora's pink chairs on either side of the picture window. Jackson spoke first.

"I want you to come home with me—stay a few days, at least until after the funeral."

"Thanks, Jackson. That's mighty nice of you to offer, but Dora's mother's driving down from Dallas tonight." Ron drained his drink and set the glass down on the table between them. "I'll be okay, I guess." He spread his hands in a gesture of hopelessness. "It's just that I don't know how I'll cope without Dora. You know how she was. She'd never let me do anything. Said I was klutzy. Hell, I don't even know how to operate the damn coffeepot. Who would have done a thing like this, Jackson?"

"As far as the sheriff's concerned, you're the prime suspect."

"Me? They think I killed my wife?"

Jackson got up and went to the kitchen to refill their glasses. When he came back he said, "Think about it. You were the last to see her alive. You had a motive. Everyone in town knew Dora was hell on wheels to live with." He set down his drink, ignoring Ron's shocked expression. "Now, here's your problem, buddy. Whoever did it tried to cover up the crime by laying her out on that towel. It's almost like they were showing some kind of sick respect for the body. That doesn't sound like a burglar caught in the act, and it doesn't sound like a random killing. It sounds like someone who knew her. Understand?"

Ron put his head in his hands.

"Could anyone besides yourself have had it in for her? Anyone else she was even close to?"

"No. Well, she played bridge, you know, so there were her friends at the club. And the women in her aerobics class."

"Anyone else?"

"Only the preacher, Brother Steve, she called him." Ron's tone flattened. "She was always talking to him on the phone about church work. You know, she was on the Board of Deacons. That took up a lot of her time."

Jackson slowly sipped his drink. "These are tough questions, but I've got to ask. There's talk around town you've been fooling around with Muriel Bonnet. Any truth in that?"

The other man's knuckles turned white against his glass. "A little." When Jackson failed to comment, he continued. "Okay, I screwed her a few times last winter. So what? I'm not the only one, for Christ's sake.''

Jackson felt his jaw tighten. ''Anything else you want to tell me?''

Ron got to his feet and began to pace the room. Finally, he stopped in front of the fireplace and faced Jackson. ''Nothing. God, I can't believe they think I did it. Help me, Jackson.''

Jackson took out a cigar, then, seeing no ashtrays in the room, put it back in his pocket. ''Did you kill her?'' He eyed Ron Hughes.

Ron put both hands on the arms of Jackson's chair and leaned toward him. ''I didn't do it, Jackson. I swear it.''

''I'll do what I can.'' Jackson picked up both their glasses and walked back into the kitchen. He dropped the glasses in the dishwasher, then opened the door under the sink and retrieved a box of dishwasher detergent. He filled the receptacle inside the machine and closed the door, turning the dial until he heard water running.

''Jackson, there's something else.'' Ron had followed him into the kitchen.

Jackson turned to face him. ''You'd better tell me.''

''It's about Muriel. I feel bad. You see, it was more than screwing her. Now don't laugh—but I was… am…in love with her.''

Jackson's lips formed a tight line. ''Why would I laugh?'' He was thinking Muriel was far too good for the likes of Ron.

''There's more.'' Ron leaned against the counter

and folded his arms. "I told Dora about it the night before she died—told her I wanted a divorce. She…well, you know how Dora was…she laughed at me."

Back home in his study, Jackson debated his decision to help the guy. Family or not, Ron Hughes was a worm. Still, he thought, even a worm has rights. He frowned and looked at his watch. Almost six-thirty. Patty would be at band practice until after eight. He picked up the remote from the table beside him and flicked on the television. Might as well watch the news before going into the kitchen to warm his supper.

THE NEXT MORNING when Jackson stepped outside to get the paper, a clap of thunder caught him unawares, and a gust of wind almost pulled the paper out of his hand. Soon the rain began in earnest, first in heavy drops that made craters in the dust, then in sheets, gushing out the end of the downspouts and carving gullies in the patchy yard as it poured into the street below. Jackson took a deep breath, enjoying the scent of the rain, then went back inside.

Patty was sitting at the kitchen table eating cold cereal. *Catcher in the Rye* was propped up against her milk glass. "Boy, was this kid a dork," she said, not taking her eyes off the page.

"I thought he was pretty cool when I was a kid." Jackson poured coffee into his favorite mug. "Did you know it was raining?"

"Raining? Oh, great! Today's the day they're having the ribbon-cutting for the new Main Street offices.

The band's supposed to play!'' Patty took a sip of milk. ''What do they do over there, anyway?''

Jackson flipped on the small television on the counter and keyed the remote to the weather station. ''It's a state-sponsored program designed to help small towns. I'm not sure exactly what they do, but I guess we'll find out as time goes by.'' He peered at the set, then turned it off. ''Just isolated showers. They should move on off by eleven. What time's the ceremony? I might walk over to hear you play.''

''We play at eleven-thirty.'' Patty got up and dropped a slice of white bread into the toaster. ''Toast?'' She looked at Jackson. When he nodded, she dropped in another slice. ''Come if you want to. Yeah, do come. We've gotten a whole lot better since the last time you heard us.''

Later, at the office, Jackson leaned against the scarred oak window frame as he scouted the scene below, noting that the maple trees on the courthouse lawn had turned a fiery red. Beyond that, the steeple of the Catholic church stood white against the blue sky. Morgan Smith, owner of the hardware store on the corner, had stored away the lawn chairs, barbecue pits, and garden hoses and replaced them with leaf rakes, space heaters, and shiny brass fireplace tools. Across the street, members of the junior-high band made their way in chattering groups toward the Main Street office dressed in their brand-new black and gold uniforms. Jackson grinned as he saw Sonny Smart and Patty walking side by side with their heads together. True to Jackson's prediction, the rain had passed, and thin white clouds scudded across the sky.

Already, a crowd was gathering for the ribbon-cutting. He glanced across the street toward the yellow bungalow that housed the Main Street offices. As he watched, the door opened and a young woman came outside to water the pots of geraniums on either side of the front door. She was tall and slender and wore a white dress. As she turned her head, he could see a gleam of gold from the hoops she wore in her ears.

He turned from the window, sat down at his desk, stared at the ceiling for a moment, then reached for the phone. He pushed the intercom button and, when Edna's voice answered, said, "Get me Frank Lee Harley on the phone. He's a trial lawyer in Houston. The number should be on my Roladex."

"Well, sh—heck, Jackson. I know who he is. Hell, he was on Larry King just last month. How do you know him, anyway?"

"Went to law school with him. Buzz me when you get him on the line."

When the buzzer sounded, Jackson picked up the phone. "How's the richest barrister in Baghdad on the Bayou?"

"Couldn't be better, Jackson. How about you? Still stiffing the yokels?"

"I'll never tell!"

"We've still got room in the firm, if you ever decide to leave Hooterville."

"Not going to happen, pal. I'm just a simple country lawyer."

"Right. Last time I heard that, I lost my shirt, shoes, and half my hair!"

Jackson chuckled. "Well, that won't happen this time. However, I think I've got something you might be interested in. My sister-in-law's been killed—murdered. It looks like her husband is shaping up to be the prime suspect."

"Oh, hey, Jackson. I'm sorry—"

"Don't be," Jackson cut in. "Nobody around here is wasting any tears over Dora—or Ron, either, for that matter. He's not much, but I've got a feeling the old boy's innocent on this one. Then, too, Dora was Patty's aunt. I feel like I ought to do something. Interested?"

"Say no more," Harley cut in. "Has he got any money?"

"Plenty. The money was Dora's, but I wrote the will. He gets it all."

"Good enough for me. Send me what you've got and, after I review it, I'll fly up there."

"Will do."

Jackson hung up just as Edna appeared at the door. "Don't forget, you've got a meeting with the commissioners at ten."

"Right." Jackson glanced at his watch. "I'll be in the courtroom. Come get me at eleven. I want to go across the street to the ribbon-cutting. Patty wants me to hear the band play."

Jackson's heels clicked on the worn terrazzo floor as he walked down the hall to the county courtroom where the monthly commissioners' court meetings were held. The county was divided into six precincts, each watched over by an elected commissioner who was responsible for maintaining the roads as well as other public spaces. It was a thankless job, which paid little and asked much, yet each election year, several men ran for each spot on the court. Jackson knew that its appeal lay in the opportunities for graft it offered. Each commissioner had at his disposal the county road equipment, and this equipment was often used to build roads and ponds on farms and ranches in the county, with the commissioner pocketing the fee. For this reason, Jackson ruled the court with an iron hand, demanding receipts and documentation for every job done.

The other six men were already seated around the counsel table in front of the judge's bench when Jackson entered the courtroom. He took a seat at the head of the table and opened the file he carried.

"Morning, gentlemen."

"Morning, Jackson," Edgar Lawson said. "I've got something to say, if you don't mind."

"Shoot," Jackson said.

"We need a new grader. The one we got stays in the shop as often as not."

The other commissioners nodded.

"Can we afford one?"

Edgar drew a sheaf of papers from his overalls pocket. "I talked to Sammy James. He says the county's got the money. Right here's some figures I put together."

Jackson took the papers. "I'll go over them this afternoon. Now, anything else?"

Jesse Grimes raised his hand. "Jackson, if we don't do something about a road out there at Willow Creek, those folks are gonna ride me out of town on a rail."

"I know." Jackson extracted a letter from his file. "I've heard from the highway department. They're dragging their feet on the thing. Looks like I'm going to have to go to Austin and try to talk some sense into them."

Jesse, who was known to be hotheaded, struck the table with his fist. "Well, goddam, Jackson, go!"

Asher Pollack spoke up. "Damn straight, Jackson. Those people needed that road three years ago when the bridge washed out. We gotta get it done!"

Jackson nodded. "I know. I've already made plans to go next week. Anything else?" He looked at his watch.

The meeting droned on for another forty-five minutes, and the band had already started to play when Jackson finally walked across the street to the Main Street office.

ELEVEN

THE SUN HAD DRIED the grass and a cool breeze ruffled the branches as Jackson found a spot under a shade tree. He grinned as the junior high band hobbled through a medley of Sousa marches, and winked at Patty, whose face was contorted into a fierce frown as she concentrated on the music sheet attached to her French horn. When the last cymbal crashed, Mayor McGonigal ascended the steps to stand on the front porch, which would serve as a stage for the ceremony. He began his address to the crowd with his standard ribbon-cutting speech. The mayor was eighty-four and had been reelected to the post more times than anyone could remember. He always gave the same speech. When he remembered, he inserted the correct name of the business being honored. Other times, he tossed out names at random, frequently naming businesses long since defunct. As the speech droned on, Jackson regarded the young woman waiting her turn to speak. She wore a red and white scarf around her neck, which complemented her clear skin, black hair, and surprising green eyes. The large gold hoops on her ears would have been gaudy on most women but seemed made for her.

After the ribbon was cut, Jackson pushed his way

to the front of the crowd and stood beside Horace Kincaid, who was busily snapping pictures for next week's paper. He gave Jackson a shove.

"Stand over there by the mayor and Miz de Alejandro." He gestured with his camera. "I want all the dignitaries in this shot."

Jackson grinned and did as he was told, quickly introducing himself to the woman as Horace set up the shot.

"Welcome to Post Oak." Jackson wondered when he'd ever seen eyes so green.

"Thank you."

After Horace had his shot and the crowd began to disperse, Jackson lingered to chat with her. "Uh," he said, suddenly inarticulate, "could I buy you something to drink?"

She looked him up and down, then smiled. "Love it. But first I have to lock the office. Will you wait here, or would you like to come in?"

Jackson waited outside until she came back carrying a small red purse. They crossed Maple Street and set off down the sidewalk toward Minton's Rexall.

"Your accent is charming."

"It's almost gone." She smiled up at him. "My father's family has been in this country for many generations, but my mother's mother, who died last year, was from Chihuahua and spoke only Spanish. We always spoke it in her home—and I visited her a lot."

"You must miss your family." Jackson took her arm as they crossed the street.

"My father is dead, and I rarely see my mother." Her voice was cold.

Jackson, not knowing how to respond, remained silent.

Finally, she spoke again. "Sorry. Yes, I do miss my family, and I do miss my mother. In many ways, Hispanic families are closer than Anglos."

"I'll take your word for it. We don't have many Mexican Americans in East Texas."

"I've noticed." She smiled wryly. "Little children stare at me."

Jackson was shocked. "You're kidding!"

"Yes, I'm kidding. Let's go in, shall we?"

Jackson held open the heavy glass door, then followed her into Minton's Drugstore, silently congratulating himself for bringing her here, away from the prying eyes at the Wagon Wheel.

"What would you like?" He guided her to a rear booth.

She looked around her. "This reminds me of the old-fashioned pharmacy in my home town of Victoria," she said. "Could I please have an ice-cream sundae?"

"Coming up," he said. "I'll join you."

He strode toward the fountain, then turned back, grinning foolishly. "I forgot to ask what flavor."

"Chocolate. With whipped cream and a cherry on top."

Jackson went to the front and gave the teenager behind the counter their orders, then watched while she scooped large dips of vanilla ice cream into lily-shaped sundae glasses and poured on thick, dark chocolate syrup. Last, she shook the whipped cream dispenser and squirted a generous amount on each sundae, finishing with a red cherry. She put them on a tray along with spoons, glasses of ice water, and napkins and pushed it toward Jackson.

Back at the table, they both dug into their sundaes.

"I feel like a kid again." Jackson talked with his mouth full. "I don't know when I last had one of these."

"It's a good thing to be a kid." She smiled. "I try to do it often."

Jackson flashed a grin and nodded in agreement. "Tell me, why did you come to East Texas?"

"It was the challenge. I had been with the Texas Historical Commission since graduating from the university working on grants, heritage tourism—that sort of thing. I wanted to get away from all the paper-shuffling and work directly on a project. When this job came up, I jumped at it." She blotted her lips with her napkin. "I believe in the Main Street Program. It has been the salvation of many a small town."

"In what way?" Jackson thought her answer had come too glibly and wondered if there might be another reason she had wanted to leave Austin.

"In a lot of ways." She pushed her dish away and leaned her arms on the table. "Texas folks come from many ethnic backgrounds. You have your Hispanics in south Texas, then the Germans came and settled the hill country, and the Cajun people from Louisiana have spilled over into many southeast Texas communities." She tapped the table with one tiny red fingernail. "The coastal towns have their own special flavor, too. But the modern world is stealing away their uniqueness. Unless something is done, Texas will become one generic freeway, dominated by fast-food joints and discount stores, not to mention the billboards and strip malls." She smiled. "Sorry. I get a little carried away at times."

"And what heritage do you hope to preserve in these parts? The Bubba factor?"

"What do you mean?"

"I mean the only ethnicity I see around here are rednecks driving pickup trucks."

She laughed. "So it's Anglo-Saxon. Does that make it any less valuable?"

"I guess not. But don't you think it's a little too late? You can't stop progress."

"I know that—and who would want to?" She took a sip of ice water. "But we can preserve what's left. I believe we can have the best of both—tradition, preserved and living in harmony with the modern world. Okay, I'll stop now. Tell me about yourself."

"No." He held up his hand. "Please, I'm interested."

"You're sure?"

He nodded.

"Each year, the Texas Historical Commission selects a few Texas cities as official Texas Main Street cities. These towns are eligible to receive certain funds as well as services to be used in a number of ways."

"Such as?"

"Oh, well, for instance, we work with communities on such things as economic development, we help downtown merchants with window display, and the owners of the buildings with architectural elements. We provide facade drawings and encourage them to preserve the integrity of the original building design. I'll bet you've seen lots of nineteenth century buildings that have been *modernized*.''

Jackson grinned. ''They look like very old ladies wearing miniskirts.''

''Right. It's like putting a stainless steel front door on Westminster Abbey.'' She took a sip of water.

''I don't think you can compare Post Oak, Texas, with Westminster Abbey.''

She smiled. ''Maybe you're right. Anyway, cities with populations under five thousand are only eligible for a part-time Main Street manager. Post Oak has sixty-four hundred, so I'm able to work full-time on the project.''

Jackson listened, hypnotized, more by the sound of her voice and the way her lips curved than by her words. He was startled when she looked at her watch and said, ''Oh, my! How could I have run on for so long? I have to go.''

Back at the courthouse, he had a hard time concentrating on the papers on his desk. His eyes kept wandering to the little yellow house across the street.

TWELVE

MYRTICE RICE SAT at the marble-topped dresser in the bedroom she had shared with her husband for so long. How many years had it been? Sometimes she had to strain to remember. Fifty-one? Or was it fifty-two? They had stopped acknowledging anniversaries long ago. She slowly removed the delicate net from her hair and began to pluck out the hairpins, placing each in a china dish. With the removal of the last pin, her hair tumbled in snowy waves past her shoulders. She picked up a silver brush and began to brush, one, two, three. Every night, she counted brush strokes until she reached one hundred, just as her mother had done, and her mother before that. Sometimes she thought enviously about her contemporaries who had their hair cut and permed at the Clip and Curl. Of course, that was out of the question for her.

Across the hall, the door to the black-and-white-tiled bathroom stood ajar. She heard Ray brushing his teeth at the sink, then urinating in the toilet. She wondered if he would flush. He didn't. She sighed. Ray had decided it was extravagant to flush every time. Once a day was enough, he decreed. And only yesterday, she had caught him going through the tiny can of kitchen garbage. When she'd asked why, he had made an excuse about losing something, but she knew he was checking on her, imagining she was being extravagant with her cooking.

She stood up and walked to the window that looked out over the back yard. She peered outside. A full moon made the ground silvery gray. She could see the shadows of the redbud trees swaying in the breeze and the tangle of wisteria that had long ago broken its arbor and now spilled haphazardly across the lawn. Something moved in the edge of the shadows. Perhaps it was the cat. She drew the drapes, thinking she'd go out and have another look for the poor thing first thing in the morning. Myrtice removed her dressing gown, placing it at the foot of the bed, then turned down the covers and crawled between the sheets. Her breathing was slow and regular when her husband climbed in beside her.

Myrtice later told the police she had no idea what time it was when she heard the bump downstairs. It startled her out of a deep sleep and for a moment she thought it was only a dream. She lay there staring up into darkness for a while, then turned on her side and tried to go back to sleep, but sleep wouldn't come. She remembered slowly adjusting herself to a more comfortable position, being careful not to wake Ray. A few minutes later she smelled the smoke. Faint at first, then its acrid scent burning her eyes and throat. She shook her husband awake and ran to the stairs. Smoke was boiling out from under the pocket doors that led to the dining room. Calling loudly to her husband to get up, she ran downstairs, picked up the phone on the hall table, and reported the fire. Gesturing wildly to her husband to follow, she pulled open the heavy front door. Glancing back at him, she saw to her horror that he had grabbed his chest and crumpled to the floor at the foot of the stairs. Myrtice ran to him and called his name, but he only moaned. Looking back toward the dining room, she saw tongues of flame darting under the door and blackening the polished hall floor. Desperately, she grabbed her husband's feet and tugged at his body. At first it didn't budge, then, gradually, inch by inch, panting from the effort, she pulled him out the door and collapsed on top of him on the concrete front porch.

The sky was turning gray through the open windows when Myrtice found herself seated in the library, coffee cup in hand, answering questions. The fire chief lounged against the grand piano writing out his report. The sheriff looked uncomfortable on her grandmother's Chippendale sofa. Fire Marshal Reynolds sat opposite her on the ottoman asking questions. Mae Applewaite, who had come over from next door to help out, came bustling into the room bringing fresh coffee and a plate of hot muffins she'd brought from home. The ambulance had left after the EMS crew revived Ray and checked his heart. They had urged him to come to the hospital for further observation but to no avail. He now sat ashen-faced in his Morris chair near the fireplace.

Marshal Reynolds put down his clipboard. "Mrs. Rice," he said, "I don't know how to say this but straight out. The fire was set."

Myrtice felt a shiver pass through her body. She looked at her husband.

"Set? You mean somebody did this on purpose?" Ray Rice set down his coffee cup with a clatter. "That's not possible. We were in the house all night. Nobody could have come in and done such a thing without our knowing."

"I could show you." Reynolds was emphatic. "But it's been a long night. Let me just say that the fire started on the breakfast room floor. Folks, fires just don't start in the middle of a hardwood floor without some incendiary material nearby—like drapes or oily rags. See what I mean?" He looked from husband to wife, then continued. "Most house fires are electrical in origin. They will start in the walls or around an electrical outlet—but never on the floor. It was pretty messed up. You'll have to get somebody out here to repair the damage. Hal Murphy's a pretty good carpenter. Want me to send him around?"

"Not at all!" Ray's voice trembled. "We'll manage." He sank back in the chair and spoke in a whisper. "Why would anyone want to set our house on fire?"

The sheriff spoke up. "That's what we want to find out, Mr. Rice. There were traces of a flammable liquid in the room—and my deputy found an empty gas can out behind the smokehouse. I'm taking that in for fingerprints." He rose to his feet. "In the meantime, why don't you folks try to get a little rest. Do you reckon you and your wife could come to the courthouse this afternoon so we can talk some more about this?"

"Of course," Myrtice answered.

"Good. Why don't you meet me at Judge Crain's office around three. Oh, by the way, the deputy found a dead cat out behind the smokehouse. It was pretty torn up. I reckon dogs must have got after it. Anyway, he disposed of it for you."

Myrtice helped Mae gather up coffee cups. "We'll be there, Sheriff. And, Mae, we thank you from the bottom of our hearts."

"Don't you think a thing about it." Mae ran hot water into the granite dishpan. "You just go on up to bed. I'll finish up here."

Later, as she hung the wet towel over the edge of the wire dish drainer, her mind was busy with plans to marshal the ladies to organize a cleaning crew to tackle the mess in the dining room. It was a cinch that old skinflint would never let go of a dime to pay anybody to do it.

THIRTEEN

THE BODY WAS RELEASED on Thursday, a week later, and Dora's funeral was held at the First Baptist Church the next day.

Ron entered the church with his mother, Patty's grandmother. Odd, Jackson thought, Dora had acted the role of aunt to Patty and sister to Gretchen so well that few remembered it was Ron who was related to them by blood and not Dora. Jackson and Patty eased into the second pew marked with a white bow to show it was reserved for family members.

The residents of Post Oak turned out in full force, more from curiosity, Jackson thought, than out of respect for Dora. No one could remember when a prominent member of the community had died in such a way. Everyone was curious to see how Ron was taking it.

The Rices had stayed home because they were still recovering from the shock of the fire.

Brother Steve took as the text for his sermon a passage from Job: "He shall return no more to his house, neither shall his place know him anymore." Vanessa, sitting on the front row wearing a sundress with a lacy scarf around her shoulders, wished he had chosen a more cheerful passage, although she had to admit it was appropriate.

The back pews held a sprinkling of the couple's friends from the country club, but the majority were there out of curiosity. Almost everyone believed Ron was guilty, and they wanted to get a good look at him before he was carted off to Huntsville.

The sheriff and Dooley Burns occupied the back pew. When the service was over, they kept their seats while the undertaker's men wheeled the casket out the door and loaded it onto the hearse. Sheriff Gibbs studied every face as the mourners filed out of the church. One person caught his attention and he surreptitiously withdrew a small pad from his shirt pocket and made a notation in it.

Outside the church, the people gathered in small groups, talking softly to each other. Edna moved from group to group, expressing the view that a man was innocent until proven guilty.

Jackson and Patty rode to the cemetery in the limousine with Ron and his mother.

Ron's mother, Geraldine, dabbed her eye with a lace handkerchief. "Funerals always make me cry. It's the music, I think. I don't pretend to grieve for Dora. Everybody knew we hated each other's guts." She batted her fake eyelashes at Jackson. "I guess you think I'm awful, Jackson."

"Not at all." Jackson wasn't going to admit it, but he did think his mother-in-law was awful, always had. It was a mystery to him how a woman like that had ever produced a kind and delicate creature like Gretchen. Geraldine Hughes was the type of female that brought out the worst in him. He looked with distaste at the thinning and permed red hair, the blue eyes faded to gray and red-rimmed, and the too-white powder caked in the wrinkles around her mouth, etched there no doubt by the long brown cigarettes she favored.

She smiled, revealing large yellow teeth, and leaned toward him, whispering conspiratorially, "Ronnie doesn't know it yet, but I've decided to stay on indefinitely. He needs a woman to take care of him." She placed her finger to her lips and looked toward her son, who was sitting in the front seat chatting with the driver. "He's helpless as a baby, you know. It's that woman. She wouldn't let him lift a finger around her precious house. I brought him up right, then she came along and messed him up." She cracked the window next to her and lit a cigarette. "And that's not the half of it, Jackson. I know butter wouldn't melt in her mouth when she was around you and Patty, but I'll bet you don't know much about her past. Did you know she was adopted?"

"Yes," Jackson lied. He wasn't going to encourage the woman.

Geraldine Hughes persisted. "Well, I had her investigated before Ronnie married her. Her birth family was—well, not our kind of people."

"She never talked much about her background," Jackson said, sneaking a glance at Ron, who was looking out the window.

"I don't doubt it. The woman put on airs like you wouldn't believe."

Jackson sat back in his seat, hoping to silence the

woman, and looked out the window as the limo proceeded slowly toward the old cemetery. The wind had picked up and the gum trees gave up their leaves in swirls of orange and red. Cattle in the fields stood with their backs to the wind, a sure sign a cold snap was on the way. It had been a day similar to this when Jackson first met Geraldine Hughes. They had driven up Interstate 35 from Austin to Dallas in his Mustang, Gretchen, small and bespectacled, beside him.

"We have to do this," she had said.

"I know."

"I wish we didn't." She spoke fiercely. "I wish you never had to meet them."

He covered her hand with his. "Gretchen, I'm not marrying your family."

"She'll want to give us some horrible pretentious wedding so she can fulfill all her stupid social obligations. We won't have a thing to say about it. You'll see."

"Then we'll elope."

Following Gretchen's directions, Jackson turned onto Central Expressway and drove north. "Turn at Mockingbird," she said.

They followed Mockingbird Lane until, passing the bustling SMU campus, they turned onto a quiet street of giant oak trees and impressive homes. Jackson glanced at Gretchen. "Keep going," she said. "There. That's it."

She pointed to a tiny house built of brick and painted gunmetal gray set back on a lot barely sufficient to hold the structure. White shutters surrounded the windows. The front door was topped with a massive scrolled pediment. Jackson stared, amazed.

"Isn't it ghastly? It's my mother's idea of elegance. They could own a nice house in a subdivision somewhere, but Mum insists on living in Highland Park." Jackson knew Highland Park was the most prestigious neighborhood in Dallas.

Geraldine had met them at the door with the ever-present cigarette in hand and dressed in a caftan of teal green lavishly trimmed with gold braid. Gold sandals and arms laden with clinking bracelets completed the outfit.

"Come in, darlings," she said. "I've made a pitcher of chi-chi's. It's the latest thing in drinks. Too yummy, really. You have to be careful, though." She rolled her eyes at Jackson. "You can hardly taste the alcohol, they're so sweet."

Jackson winced.

She led them into a minuscule living room crammed to the rafters with large furniture. Soon Jackson and Gretchen found themselves seated side by side on a brocaded sofa clutching icy drinks, listening and nodding as Geraldine spoke loudly and excitedly about the coming wedding.

"I thought St. Michael and All Angels for the ceremony. Such a lovely sanctuary. And the reception at the Mansion at Turtle Creek."

"Mother, you can't afford that. What will Daddy say?"

"Oh, who cares? He'll just have to cash in some of those bonds he has. You're his only daughter, and he adores you. Besides, Jackson needs to make contacts here in the city.'' She looked at Jackson. "Have you decided what firm you're going with? Billison, Billison and Murphy is the best, I hear.''

Jackson cleared his throat. "Mrs. Hughes, I'm not joining a Dallas law firm. I plan to go back to my home town, Post Oak.''

"Oh, my dear, you can't do that. Why, that's professional suicide.''

Gretchen set her drink firmly on the glass-topped coffee table and got to her feet. "Can I help with lunch, Mum? Something smells delicious in the kitchen.''

One week after graduation, Jackson and Gretchen, with their friends Tim and Mary Glover as witnesses, drove to Louisiana and married in a small bayou church.

"Jackson!" Jackson was jolted out of his reverie. "Don't you agree that Dora looked better dead than she ever did alive?''

"Mother!" Ron was shocked.

Geraldine giggled and lit another cigarette. "Well, she does.''

Jackson was relieved to see the limo turn down the tree-lined lane that led to the cemetery.

LATER THAT EVENING, Jackson and Patty sat in the den enjoying the first fire of the season. They hadn't eaten the supper Lutie Faye had left because they had both stuffed themselves at the reception following the funeral. Patty, curled up on one end of the couch, legs tucked beneath her, stretched and yawned.

"If I never have to go to another funeral, it'll be too soon."

Jackson looked at her fondly. Indeed, he thought, thirteen was much too young to have seen so much of death. He couldn't think of an answer, so he said nothing.

"Daddy, who do you reckon killed Aunt Dora? Do you think it's somebody we know?"

"Don't know, honey. But we'll find out." Jackson lit a Don Diego and flipped the spent kitchen match into the fire. "I imagine it was just some transient looking for somebody to rob."

"Did he take anything?" She knitted her brows, looking at Jackson.

"Well, not that we know of. Uncle Ron has been too upset to really search the house fully."

Patty made a face. "That reminds me. Gramma says I have to come out there and help her go through Aunt Dora's stuff. Do I have to?"

"Do you really hate the idea?"

"I guess not. I guess I ought to help out. Gramma and Uncle Ron said I could have anything I wanted— like I would want any of her old stuff."

Jackson got up and threw another log on the fire.

"Daddy."

"Hmmm?"

"What do you do when you know somebody likes you, and you don't like them back?"

Jackson's eyebrows arched upward. "Who is it?"

"Sonny Smart."

"The newspaper boy?" Jackson remembered how his paper always landed directly in front of the house and smiled. "Well, I'd just be nice to him. He'll get over it eventually."

"Easy enough for you to say." Patty got off her chair and started toward the front door. "You don't have him following you around all day long. It's enough to make a person... Oh, well, I'll figure something out. I'm hungry." She flounced out of the room, leaving Jackson to smile into the fire, thinking how great it would be to be that young again.

FOURTEEN

THE NEXT MORNING was Saturday. Jackson came down the back stairs wearing a long-sleeved plaid shirt and corduroy trousers. When he went out to get the paper, the wind was icy and a light frost had formed in the shade of the big house. Sonny had missed the porch this time, so the newspaper lay on the grass. His feet left prints on the frosty ground as he walked to retrieve it. The leaves of the crepe myrtle in the side yard were beginning to be tipped with red. The sun was just rising over the peaked roof of the Boyd house across the street. He stood and watched as Ham Boyd opened the door to let out the dog. The dog, Shandy, quickly raised his leg at the mock orange tree beside the steps before beginning his morning patrol of the yard, nose to the ground. Fall was here, and Jackson felt energized, even though he was well aware that the temperature would rise into the eighties by midafternoon.

He went into the kitchen and, reaching into the pantry, retrieved the loaf of homemade bread Lutie Faye had baked the day before. He cut off two thick slices and buttered them generously before sliding them into the oven to toast, then poured himself a cup of coffee and sat down at the kitchen table to read the paper.

He tried to concentrate on the local news, but his mind kept wandering. First he thought about Ron's mother and her evil tongue. What a disgusting woman. Next, his thoughts turned to Mandy de Alejandro and stayed there. Maybe he'd just invite her over for dinner sometime. He could barbecue steaks and throw together a decent salad. He thought about her lilting voice and the unexpected inflections that made music of her words. He was enchanted by her creamy skin and full expressive lips, her green eyes that danced when she spoke excitedly about her work. He put his chin in his hand and thought about what it would be like to hold her in his arms. Just as he was about to kiss her passionately, he smelled something. His toast! He jerked open the oven door and coughed as smoke billowed out. Grabbing a dishtowel, he pulled the toast out and dumped it into the sink, cursing himself for his foolishness.

"Pee-yew." Patty came into the kitchen wearing one of Jackson's huge T-shirts.

Jackson opened the window, then the kitchen door. "Your daddy's a dope."

"Nah," she said. "Want me to make you some more?"

"I'm out of the mood." He picked up the toast and tossed it into the trash. "Think I'll go out and load the woodbox. What are you doing today?"

Patty was rummaging through the refrigerator. She pulled out a jar of homemade jam. "A bunch of us are riding our bikes out to the canyon for a picnic. Mind?"

The canyon was not a canyon at all, but a large dry creek bed in the woods just outside of town.

"Not if you go with a crowd." Jackson drained his coffee cup. "Just don't ever go out there alone."

"No way," Patty said. "That would be too spooky."

After Patty had peddled off down the street, picnic lunch in a plastic grocery sack slung over her handlebars, Jackson put on his black windbreaker and went out the back door to tackle the woodpile. His feet crunched on the gravel pathway and he made his way to the toolshed, which, in his grandmother's time, had been a smokehouse. The door was held shut by the simple means of a wooden block attached to the facing with a nail. He rotated the block and, lifting from the bottom, tugged open the door, then, reaching up, pulled the string that hung from a single bulb suspended from the ceiling by a frayed electric cord. Evidence that rats were in residence dusted the floor like large grains of black rice. He glanced around the confusion of Patty's old crib and high chair, a rusty tricycle, boxes spilling over with broken appliances and discarded pots and pans. Against the wall hung the leaf rake and hoe along with Gretchen's old gardening hat and gloves. Her rubber gardening boots, tiny and crusted with mud, rested in the corner by the door. He edged his way to the rear wall and the workbench that had once belonged to his grandfather. Resting on its top he found saws, hammers, and the axe he was seeking. He picked up the axe and ran his finger across the blade. Dull, of course. Next, pawing through the mess, he found a grinding stone, which he attached to the vise on the bench. He ground the blade across the stone, not stopping until its edge was razor-keen. He took the axe to the woodpile behind the shed and split two wheelbarrow loads, which he loaded into the box beside the back porch. Then, sweating, he took off his jacket and rolled up the sleeves of his shirt. He glanced around the yard. Forgetting that he had planned to tackle the new John Grisham novel today, he went back to the shed and took out the lawn mower, dusty from disuse. He fueled it up, added oil, and set to work on the grass. It was noon before he stood gazing at his handiwork. Pleased, he went into the house to eat a sandwich. He poured himself a glass of iced tea and took his lunch to the seldom-used sunroom, where he sat down beside a wicker table by the window.

He felt good, energized by the physical labor. So good, in fact, that he decided to start trimming the overgrown privet hedge that was threatening to take over the back patio. He was halfway down the length of it when he heard Patty calling from the street.

"Daddy! Where are you?"

Jackson walked around the side of the house and found Patty and Sonny Smart racing up the drive. As one, they dropped their bikes, ran his way, and stood panting in front of him.

"What?" Jackson suppressed a grin.

"Not funny, Daddy," Patty said, irritated not to be taken seriously. "We saw a man. Ooh, he was scary. Tell him, Sonny."

"Yes, sir," Sonny said. "He had a beard and was all dirty—"

"Like the Unibomber," Patty added helpfully. "And Daddy, he'd made himself a camp out at the canyon. It was gross; he'd killed a bunch of animals and stuff."

"And hung their hides up in the trees to dry," Sonny said.

"Where are the other kids?" Jackson asked.

"Gone home, I guess. When that dude came charging out of the woods, we were so scared we, like, all jumped on our bikes and got out of there."

"Well, why don't you go in the house and cool down," Jackson said. He took Patty's chin in his hands. "And I don't ever want you going out there again."

"Huh," Patty said, turning toward the house, "like I'd ever want to!"

That night, after supper, Jackson said, "I thought you didn't like Sonny Smart."

Patty blushed. "I didn't say I didn't like him exactly. I just said I wished he wouldn't follow me around all the time." She pleated the hem of her T-shirt. "He's okay, I guess."

After Patty had gone upstairs for her bath, Jackson picked up the phone. He dialed Mandy's number and, when she answered, invited her for dinner the following night. He set down the receiver with a satisfied smile, then, picking up the neglected John Grisham novel, climbed the stairs for a nap before supper.

FIFTEEN

THE FELLOWSHIP HALL of First Baptist was a large room with a door at one end, windows along the sides, and a kitchen at the other end. Beneath the windows, folded chairs and tables rested in readiness for the next church social. Beside the kitchen wall stood a bookshelf holding what Brother Steve called the "Church Library," a collection of seldom-read inspirational books and five or six dog-eared Bibles placed there for anyone who chose to take one. The green-painted walls were adorned with children's artwork left over from Vacation Bible School. Today, under the chairmanship of Mae Applewaite, the ladies of the church met in the fellowship hall for thirty minutes between Sunday School and church to discuss the annual fall rummage sale and barbecue, which was to be held in October. The church rummage sale was eagerly awaited by a large number of Post Oak's less fortunate, as it gave them an opportunity to stock up on children's clothing and household items at greatly reduced prices. Everyone else looked forward to eating barbecue with all the trimmings in the large parklike lawn behind the church.

This year, the ladies were faced with a crisis. Dora Hughes, who had chaired the event for the past five years, was now dead, and nobody had a clue what to do. Dora had been such an efficient organizer that the others had all sat back and waited while she gave each member specific instructions as to what was expected of her.

"I could have told you this was going to happen," boomed Jane Archer. "The woman was a control freak—God rest her soul."

"Jane!" gasped her sister, Esther.

"Words can't hurt her now, sister." Jane adjusted her girdle.

"We can store the donations in an empty jail cell just like last year," offered Norma Jean Gibbs, the sheriff's wife. "And I'll be glad to price everything if somebody'll help me."

Several people offered to help, and Norma Jean wrote down their names.

Vanessa raised her hand. "I'll be glad to do the table decorations."

"It's a barbecue outside." Jane vetoed the idea. "We don't need decorations."

"Well, I thought just clay pots with a few red flowers…"

"That's very nice, Vanessa." Mae Applewaite spoke in a loud voice. She felt she was losing control of the meeting. "Now, who did the merchandise tables last year?"

"I did," volunteered Annabeth Jones. "Mae, you helped. Remember?"

The debate went on until every lady had a job. Mae thought they had covered everything, but said a little prayer just in case. She was about to adjourn the meeting when Jane spoke up.

"Aren't you forgetting something, Mae?"

Mae looked at Jane with raised eyebrows.

"You know, the Rices. Remember?"

"My stars! I did forget." Mae held up her hands for silence. "Ladies, I guess everybody here knows about the fire over at the Rice mansion. The damage is pretty much confined to the dining room, but that room's a real mess. Now, as Christians, I was thinking—"

"You're right, Mae." The voice came from somewhere in the back.

"Absolutely."

"It's a dead-dog cinch he's not going to pay to have it done." This from Edna in the front row. "Who wants to volunteer to help out?"

Several women raised their hands and it was decided to go that very afternoon, Sunday or not.

Now Brother Steve stood up and stepped to the front. "Ladies, let's all bow our heads and have a brief prayer for the success of our sale as well as for our brethren, the Rices."

At the end of the prayer, Mae adjourned the meeting.

"Oh, look," remarked Esther, as they crossed the grassy strip between the Fellowship Hall and church. "There's Jackson Crain and Patty. I don't know when I've seen them in church. Certainly not since Gretchen died."

"Well, it sure is." Jane stood on tiptoe to see. "And look, there's that woman from the Main Street offices. I thought all Mexicans were Catholics. Will wonders never cease!"

SIXTEEN

THE COALS WERE HOT, the potatoes in the oven, and a large salad waited on the counter when Mandy de Alejandro tapped on the front door. A bottle of good red wine stood open on the table. Jackson had offered to fetch her in his car, but she insisted on walking the short distance from her little rent house to the Crain house. He caught his breath when he opened the door. She was the most beautiful creature Jackson had seen in a long time. She was dressed in a simple sundress that hugged her curves in all the right places. The dress was white with narrow piping the color of the turquoise and silver jewelry that dangled from her ears and caressed the honey curve of her throat. Her green eyes had taken on the color of the stones and reminded Jackson of the water he'd seen off the coast of Acapulco on some long-ago vacation.

The early cold snap had passed, so they sat in lawn chairs in the newly mowed back yard while Jackson tended the steaks and tried not to stare too blatantly at her.

"How do you like your steak?" He picked up one of the sizzling ribeyes with his tongs and held it up for her to see.

"Medium rare."

"Good. Me, too. I think they're almost ready. If you would just hand me the plates…"

They carried their plates to the sunroom, where Jackson had set the wicker table with a red-checked cloth. He had found candles in the sideboard in the dining room and set them in Gretchen's glass holders. While they ate, he tried not to look too often at Mandy. He couldn't help thinking she looked like an Aztec princess, with the candlelight, like ancient ceremonial fires, playing across her face.

After the dishes were cleared away, he poured the Kona coffee he'd bought at the gift shop that day into the brand-new coffee grinder he'd also purchased and made a fresh pot of the aromatic brew.

"Hmm, heaven." She smiled as she sipped her coffee. "This stuff costs a fortune. I never buy it."

"Tell the truth, neither do I," Jackson said. "This is my first dinner party on my own."

"Then I'm honored. Shall we sit on the front porch?"

Jackson led the way to the porch and they both took a seat on the swing. Jackson didn't know what to do with the arm that rested next to her, so he threw it over the back of the seat. He was amazed when she scooted closer to him. She smelled like gardenias.

Over the sound of the creaking swing, he told her about the murder and how he felt responsible for finding the killer and clearing his brother-in-law.

"What if he's guilty?" she asked.

"Then he'll have to take his lumps, of course. I don't think he did it, though. Ron's not a very admirable character, but I don't see him as a murderer."

He glanced at her profile as she stared up at the moon through the trees. "He wouldn't have the stomach for it."

"Maybe he hired someone to do it."

Jackson grinned. "You've been watching too many cop shows. This is little Post Oak, Texas. We don't have hired guns around here."

She smiled and shrugged. "You may be right. Who do you think did it?"

"No idea. The sheriff has some evidence. When we get the report back from the lab, that might tell us something. Let's talk about you."

She laughed. "Me?"

"Sure. Tell me more about the Historical Commission."

"Okay, well let me see. I've told you about the Main Street Program. In addition to that, the commission works with county historical commissions and organizations. We do a lot of work with museums, both small and large. We work with property owners to save archaeological sites on private land. We administer the state's historical marker program."

"Oh, yes, the markers," Jackson said. "They're all over the place."

"Over eleven thousand across the state. Are you really interested in all this?"

"Not really." Jackson laughed. "I just like to hear you talk. More coffee? Or wine?"

"No. It's getting late, and tomorrow's Monday. I'd better be getting home."

Jackson walked her home, then walked on air coming back. He didn't remember ever feeling this way.

He'd loved Gretchen dearly. But that was a quieter love and had grown from shared experiences during the marriage. He couldn't remember being hit by such powerful emotions so early on. He sprinted across the lawn and into the house. Tomorrow he'd give her a call. He couldn't wait to hear that voice again.

SEVENTEEN

SOMEONE HAD PUKED all over the toilet. Boogie covered her face to mask the smell and grabbed a few paper towels to cover the seat. She had to go bad and this was better than squatting behind some tree. She had escaped from the trucker at this fucking roadside park on Interstate 30 after she had kicked him hard in the groin while he was trying to rape her. Oh, well, at least he brought her all the way from Austin before deciding to go all horny on her. In a way, Boogie blamed herself for the attack. She had allowed herself to relax in the big cab while she listened to this guy going on about how he missed his wife in Laredo and his kids and all. He told her he always bought gifts for every member of the family every single time he went on a haul, even if it was for only a few days. And because she was sleep-deprived and hungry and the cab was warm, she had fallen into a pleasant trancelike state as he droned on and on. Boogie had hardly noticed when he pulled into the roadside park, all the while talking about his son's Little League team and how he was going to coach next year. She had been staring out the window thinking maybe there were families who did those things, fathers who never crept into their kids' rooms at night for a quickie and the next day beat them up just for the fun of it—and mothers who could manage to draw a sober breath, at least until noon. Then, without warning, the trucker had jumped on top of her and started tearing at her clothes. She kicked him hard as he fumbled with his belt and when he doubled up in pain, she grabbed her backpack and jumped out of the truck. Boogie sprinted to the women's restroom and slammed the door behind her. Thank God the lock wasn't broken; they were in most of these places. She stood panting against the door until she heard the big semi start up and pull out onto the highway, then walked into the stall.

When she was finished, she approached the dingy lavatory and turned on the water. Damn. The bastards had installed one of those faucets that you had to hold down to keep the water running. With one palm, she pressed the chrome button while holding her head under the flow. She splashed water on her face and up her arms. Then, looking to make sure nobody was around, she slipped out of her clothes and, using paper towels, cleaned herself all over, paying special attention to the weeping rash that had appeared on her legs after she walked across a field of nettles.

Boogie examined herself in the mirror and nodded with satisfaction. She dug into her backpack and took out a photograph, the one of her as a baby sitting on her mother's lap by the sea. That kid had chubby, baby-fat cheeks and wide, deer-in-the-headlights eyes. The photo bore only superficial resemblance to the sixteen-year-old face she examined so critically today. The eyes, no longer frightened, seemed to say with

absolute certainty that the worst the world could do
to her had already been done. The skin was unnaturally dark, dark from exposure and lack of washing.
Boogie didn't remember when she last had a real
bath. The grime seemed to have seeped through her
pores and changed the very pigment of her skin. She
ran her fingers through her hair, causing it to spike
up. It was coal-black. The name on the packet of dye
had said ''Gothic.'' Mick was into Gothic, so she'd
had it done. She pulled a stub of an eyeliner pencil
out of her bag and lined her eyes, then applied dark,
almost black, lipstick. Last, she retrieved a fresh
T-shirt from her bag and slipped it over her head. It,
too, was black. She touched the scar that ran from
just outside her right eyebrow back into her hairline
at the temple and remembered the night Mick had hit
her across the head with a wine bottle. She had had
to go to the emergency room to get sewed up, and
afterward, he had been sorry and shared half his stuff
with her. Mick had spread his bedroll behind a Dumpster in an alley off Guadalupe Street, where they had
made love under the stars. When she thought of that
night now, tried to focus on an image of Mick's face,
all she remembered was the putrid odor that perme-
ated the ground around that Dumpster.

That was the night she had promised to get the
tattoo. God, how that had hurt. Mick wouldn't be satisfied with something small on her arm or leg. Even
the boobs or belly would have been better. No, he
wanted a rope around the tender skin of her neck. And
it had to have a hangman's noose dropping down between her breasts. She fingered the tattoo and smiled.

Fuck Mick. He was locked up at Gatesville for a long time, and she was free. Not only that, she was getting out of Austin and off the streets. She was going to have a real home.

EIGHTEEN

MANDY DE ALEJANDRO walked into the Knitter's Nook on Saturday morning wearing biker shorts and running shoes. She wanted to buy some pink yarn to knit a crib blanket for her sister's new baby girl. Vanessa Largent had come in to pick up some lace for a collage she was putting together.

"Morning," Jane Archer said from behind the counter. "You're the new Main Street lady, aren't you?" Jane didn't approve of women wearing shorts on the street, but she wasn't about to offend a customer.

Mandy nodded and told Jane what she was looking for.

"Esther, come up here," Jane called over her shoulder. "Esther's the expert on knitting," she explained. "I'm more of a needlepoint person, myself. Needlepoint's simple, nothing but in and out…in and out. My fingers all turn into thumbs when I pick up a pair of knitting needles." She turned to her sister, who had come up from the back. "Esther, help this lady find some baby yarn."

While Mandy was examining the yarn, Edna Buchannan walked in carrying a shopping bag. She reached into the bag and pulled out a large naked plastic doll and set it on the counter.

"Bless Pat, what's that?" Jane propped her elbows on the counter and stared at the doll with distaste.

Edna looked at her with disbelief. "It's a goddam doll," she said.

Vanessa hid a smile.

"Well, I can see that, can't I? What'd you bring it in here for?"

"I want to crochet a dress for it to go on my granddaughter's bed," Edna said. "Let's see, I'm gonna need some red, green, and white crochet cotton—not too fine. I don't want to be all year on the damn thing."

At that moment, Mae Applewaite walked in.

"Ooh, Edna," she said. "What's the latest on the murder?" She flopped down at the little tea table the sisters had set up near the display window. "Come over here and tell me all about it."

"Well, I'm not supposed to talk about what goes on at the office." Edna abandoned the doll and went to sit beside Mae. "But I can tell you Jackson's bound and determined to prove that brother-in-law of his didn't kill his wife. If you ask me, he's wasting his time. That Ron Hughes ain't worth a dime, and he never has been."

"My, oh, my," Esther said.

"Somebody said Dora had been…you know… interfered with." Mae hated to ask, but she was dying to know.

"You mean raped?" Edna warmed to her subject.

"Hell, no. Who in his right mind would want to rape Dora Hughes?"

"A sex maniac." Esther shuddered.

"I heard she had no clothes on. That right, Edna?" Jane asked.

Edna looked at her scornfully. "That's what you get for listening to street talk. She had on her bathing suit, but the top was undone. Now, that's the truth, and if you say it came from me, I'll say you lied. Judge would be mad if he thought I'd talked out of school—which I'd never do in a thousand years, of course."

"Of course," Mae soothed. "It'll probably all be in the paper eventually anyway."

Mandy paid for her purchases and went out the door, wondering if she'd made a mistake leaving Austin for the peace and quiet of the country. As she started down the sidewalk, Vanessa caught up with her.

"How about stopping in at the Wagon Wheel for lunch?" she said. "Steve's going to be at the church all day working on his sermon—and I could eat a bear."

Mandy looked into the other woman's open face and couldn't suppress a grin. "You're on. I could eat one, too."

As the two strolled down the town's brand-new brick sidewalk, Mandy thought about how she'd had to talk long and hard to get the city council to agree to put in the sidewalks, even though the state was footing half the bill. Vanessa spoke to everyone they met, including Rooster Pike's fat white bulldog,

Spike, who was having a nap in front of his owner's meat market.

Mandy and Vanessa ordered cheeseburger baskets and vanilla malts at the Wagon Wheel and dived right in.

Vanessa poured a pool of ketchup in her basket and trailed a french fry through the red goo. "Rip makes the best fries in the world," she said, popping it into her mouth. "I heard you had dinner over at Jackson's the other night."

Mandy giggled. "You've got ketchup on your chin."

"Don't try to change the subject." Vanessa wiped her chin with a paper napkin. "Do you like him? I think he's the cutest man in this town. All the women are crazy for him."

"I do like him," Mandy said. "And you're right, he's handsome, in a Gregory Peckish sort of way. "It's just that…"

"What?"

"I'm not getting involved with anyone ever again. Besides, this project will end eventually, and I'll be sent somewhere else."

"Sounds like you've got a story to tell." Vanessa popped the last of her cheeseburger into her mouth. "But I won't pry. And I do see what you mean. You don't want him falling in love with you, right?"

Mandy ducked her head. "Well…"

Vanessa reached across the table and patted her hand. "Well, honey, go with the flow. If it's meant to be—it will be."

"Is that the way it was with you?"

Vanessa sobered. "It was…and Steve and I were the happiest two people you could ever hope to meet."

"Were?"

Vanessa looked at her watch. "Oh, gee. Look at the time. I've got to pick up Steve's suit from the cleaners and they close at one on Saturday. 'Bye, hon. Call me sometime."

Mandy stared openmouthed as Vanessa hurried out the door and down the sidewalk, waving good-bye as she passed the window.

NINETEEN

FIRELIGHT CAST dancing shadows on the book-lined walls of Jackson's study as he dropped contentedly into his leather chair. The room was small, the smallest in the house, and masculine in every way except for the full-length portrait of Jackson's grandmother that hung over the mantel in its ornate gold frame. She had hung there as long as Jackson could remember, delicate in her 1920s gown and tiny pointed shoes. Soft blond hair, bobbed in the style of the day, framed her pointed face, and her eyes twinkled as if she knew a scandalous secret. Jackson had never been able to connect this vivacious girl with the Nana he had visited as a child and who had died when he was seven. He remembered his grandmother as blue-haired, corseted, and forbidding, forever admonishing him to wash his hands and be a little gentleman. The only other ornamentation in the room was the ormolu clock on the mantel and his father's Stickley desk with its Tiffany lamp. Jackson loved this room.

Patty, as usual, was at a friend's house. He picked up the phone, thinking he might just give Mandy de Alejandro a call, then put it back down. Better to call tomorrow and ask her out. But where? Post Oak had no places to go. Maybe he'd ask her to a movie and dinner over in Scottsboro. That was only forty miles away, and the drive would give them a chance to get to know each other.

He got up and made himself a drink, then sank back down in his chair. He picked up the current *Newsweek* and thumbed through it. Nothing here but bad news. He threw the magazine down and sat thinking about the murder. He had hoped some new evidence would be found to throw the sheriff off Ron's trail, but so far, none had appeared. And Ron wasn't helping matters in the least. The talk around the Wagon Wheel was that he had been seen on two separate occasions driving around in his car with Muriel in the seat beside him. Should he talk to Ron about it? Jackson shook his head. If the guy chose to be that reckless, he most likely wouldn't listen anyway.

The fire was burning low, so he threw on another log and poked it until sparks flew, then sat back down, still thinking about Ron. Patty had received a call from him the night before. When she returned to the kitchen where Jackson was drying the supper dishes, she looked distinctly irritated.

"That Uncle Ron—he's such a dweeb." Patty perched on the kitchen stool near where Jackson was standing.

Jackson wasn't sure what a "dweeb" was, but he had a feeling Patty was probably right on target. "What did he want?"

"He and Gram already went through Aunt Dora's stuff. He said Gram took most of her good jewelry, but he wants me to go out there and pick out what I want. Now, Daddy, I ask you, what would I want with any of her old stuff? I'm just a kid!''

"I agree." Jackson folded the towel and hung it over the wire dish drainer. "There's probably nothing you would want now. But think about when you're grown. She may have photographs—or letters. When you're older, you might just be interested in those things."

"I guess. But Daddy, I don't want to have to go through a dead person's stuff. It's creepy."

"Tell you what," Jackson had said. "I'll go with you."

As it turned out, when Jackson and Patty drove into Ron's driveway, three large cartons were waiting on the front porch with a note from Ron saying to take them. He had had a last-minute golf date and would not have time to stand by while Patty searched through the things. Now they were stacked in the front hall waiting to be opened. Jackson drained his drink and got up from his chair. Might as well move them up to the spare room, he thought. Maybe he could donate some of the stuff to the church rummage sale. He would help Patty go through the boxes tomorrow.

The spare bedroom had once been Gretchen's sewing room. It was the largest and lightest room in the house, with cream-painted woodwork and fading flower-sprigged wallpaper. Gretchen's machine and cutting table still occupied the space. It had not served as a bedroom, Jackson remembered, since his Gram had died there on Jackson's seventh birthday. He had only the vaguest memories of the old lady, small and quick as the canary she kept in a cage near the bay window. Sometimes he wondered whether the images of her he held in his mind were real or only gleaned from stories his mother had told. He could see her curved over her supper tray, picking up tiny morsels with hands that resembled claws, or leaning on her cane attaching an apple slice to the bars of the bird-cage. His mother told him Gram had read stories to him and that the two of them had played Old Maid together, but Jackson remembered none of that. He did remember running up the stairs on his birthday to show Gram his new red fire engine. Discovering the doctor standing beside her bed talking softly to his parents and ignoring Gram lying still and white beneath the sheet, Jackson had gone back downstairs and hidden in the closet under the stairs. Later, his father found him and told him Gram had gone to heaven to be with God. Gram's bed had been taken away after that and a new one had appeared in its place and, from time to time, visiting relatives would sleep there. But after Gretchen died, the room became the ''junk room,'' catching everything that had out-lived its usefulness to Jackson and Patty. Here were Patty's easel and paints from last summer when she had thought she wanted to take painting lessons be-cause her best friend Shelly was taking them. And leaning against the wall were her bow and quiver full of arrows. She had had to have these after she'd won a badge for archery at camp and was sure that she wanted to train for the Olympics. In one corner stood Jackson's golf clubs. He had played a little golf in his younger years, and was never quite sure he wouldn't want to take it up again. Jackson sat down on a cedar chest that held Gretchen's old clothes. What was he keeping this stuff for? Was it laziness? Or was he trying to hold on to a life that was over?

Just then, an image of Mandy flashed across his mind and the decision was made. He got off the cedar chest and opened the lid, flinching as he caught the faint scent of Gretchen still lingering there. He picked up a silk blouse and pressed it to his face, fighting an unexpected wave of emotion. Then, squaring his shoulders, he dropped it on the floor and began emptying the chest, shoving aside the memories each item held. In one pile, he put the clothes, shoes, scarves, and purses he would give to the rummage sale. In another, he put Gretchen's jewelry and the letters and photographs he thought Patty might like to keep someday. He went down the back stairs to the kitchen and, opening the cabinet door under the sink, retrieved the box of large trash bags Lutie Faye kept there. Back upstairs again, he stuffed the clothes into a bag, then carefully replaced the other items in the cedar chest. He stood and surveyed his work, feeling an inexplicable sense of lightness and renewed energy.

He decided to tackle the boxes Ron had sent. The first box contained the bright and expensive clothes Dora had favored, green, shocking pink, turquoise pantsuits and blouses, dresses and skirts covered with elaborate designer prints, delicate hand-sewn nightgowns with robes to match. Ron had shown no respect for Dora's things. Everything had been tossed randomly into the boxes as if he could not wait to get them out of the house. Jackson opened the second box and found essentially the same thing, only this time the box was full of shoes, belts, and handbags. The third box contained jars of makeup, lotions, and expensive perfumes. Jackson tossed everything into a pile ready to fill the next trash bag. Tomorrow he would borrow Edna's pickup to haul the whole mess down to the church basement. The sewing machine, archery equipment, golf clubs, and paints would go, too. Someone could be using them, Jackson thought, surprised he hadn't decided this long ago.

He loaded the trash bags and lined them all against the wall, then placed the other items nearby. It was when he was gathering up the empty boxes to take downstairs for the trash that he noticed he had overlooked something. A large manila envelope, bulging with papers, had wedged itself between the flaps in the bottom of one carton. Holding the envelope under his arm, Jackson picked up the empty cartons and took them to the back door, where he dropped them on the ground beside the steps. He would flatten them in the morning and put them in the garbage cans. He then took the envelope into the den. He poked the fire until it blazed brightly before settling comfortably in his chair to examine the contents of the envelope.

When he finally finished reading, he made himself another drink and sat for a long time staring into the fire. When at last the fire was cold and dead, Jackson went upstairs to bed. The envelope had contained Dora's adoption papers. She had been an older child when she was adopted—almost ten. Her birth records showed that her mother, one Rosa Luna, had lived in the disease- and poverty-stricken *colonias* of south Texas. Jackson and every other Texan knew the *colonias* as places where no such thing as running water existed and raw sewage emptied into open ditches where children played. These shantytowns were the shame of the Texas-Mexican border. Everybody knew it, and nobody did anything. Politicians flew down for photo ops every election year, promising to correct the problem. They never did.

So, this had been proud Dora's start in life. And she must have remembered it.

But it was not thoughts of Dora that caused Jackson to lie awake half the night. It was the name of her adoptive parents, *de Alejandro*.

TWENTY

BOOGIE RESTED under a sweet gum tree beside Farm to Market Road 21. Buzzards circled overhead, beautiful in flight yet so grotesque at rest. Boogie knew about buzzards; she had seen five once along the highway, jockeying for position around the carcass of a dog, dusty black with naked red heads, bent beaks, and sharp talons. She shuddered at the memory. She had smoked her last cigarette last night and now the craving for nicotine was intense. Don't think about it, she admonished herself. She looked around her. From the hill where she sat she could see a hay baler attached to the rear of a tractor. It was cutting the tall grass and leaving in its wake cylinder-shaped bales that dotted the valley beneath like some child's blocks carelessly tossed aside. She took a deep breath, taking in the heavenly scent of freshly mowed grass. At the far end of the pasture a pickup drove slowly, honking its horn while cows trotted eagerly behind, well schooled in the knowledge that the sound of that horn meant feeding time. Boogie raised her arms above her head and stretched. God, what she wouldn't give for a smoke. She tried to focus on the bath she'd have soon, the real bed with clean sheets. She lay back on the grass and looked at the sky through star-pointed leaves, just turning red at the tips. She would let her hair grow out natural and go back to school—or take the GED—then get a job. She'd get a waitressing job, make her own money. And she would lose the stupid nickname. Boogie had been tacked on her early in life all because her mother had the bright idea to call her Bougainvillea, after the flower. She'd change her name to Tiffany. To Boogie, "Tiffany" conjured up images of the sorority girls with their perky ponytails that bobbed up and down as they walked The Drag next to the University of Texas campus. Boogie and her friends had been invisible to them, no different from the toothless bums gathered in clusters on the sidewalk hiding their bottles in paper sacks. Maybe she'd let her hair grow long and wear it in a ponytail. For a moment the old fear made its appearance. What if they refused to take her in?

They'd have to, she told herself. She was a blood relative, wasn't she? And if they tried to refuse, well, she had her secret weapon. She'd threaten to tell what she knew—and that was plenty. Boogie closed her eyes, and before long, she was asleep, dreaming of a better life.

TWENTY-ONE

RAIN SPATTERED the courthouse windows and ran down in dirty dribbles. A gust of wind startled the pecan trees outside, sending a shower of soggy leaves swirling skyward. Fall was in the air. Jackson reluctantly pulled his eyes away from the little yellow house across the street and returned to his desk. He picked up the gold Cross pen his father had given him and forced himself to concentrate on the papers scattered in front of him. Now that the commissioners had voted to build a new farm to market road in the southern part of the county, it was Jackson's job to prepare the proper forms and personally take them to the highway department in Austin. The paperwork was the part of his job that he hated the most. He had been hard at it for an hour when Edna pushed open the door and entered the office.

"Goddam son-of-a-bitch!" she remarked, taking a seat in the leather guest chair in front of his desk.

Jackson sighed.

"Not you, Jackson," she said. "The sheriff. He just came busting into my office like a goddam tornado. Said for you to come to the jail right away. No explanations or nothing—not even a hidy-do." Edna's big hair quivered with indignation.

"I'll go see what he wants."

"Tell him he can kiss my royal..."

Jackson was out the door and down the hall before she could finish.

The sheriff and Dooley Burns were seated in the sheriff's spacious office in the front room of the jail when Jackson pushed open the door. The sheriff was frowning at a sheaf of papers in his hand. Dooley was cleaning his fingernails with a toothpick.

"What's all the excitement?" Jackson was out of breath from sprinting across the courthouse lawn.

"No excitement. Edna overreacts," Sheriff Gibbs said. "I just got the lab reports on your sister-in-law. Thought you'd be interested in the results."

"Of course."

"First the autopsy report. Says here she died from a blow to the back of the head. That's not to say she hadn't been strangled, too. Seems she had bruises on her neck and shoulders."

Jackson nodded.

"Also, her neck was broken. Report says it's consistent with being shaken—you know, real hard."

"My God!" Jackson said.

"Yeah."

"What about the other evidence? Had she put up a fight?"

The sheriff squinted at the report. "Hmm. No, clothes intact—no human tissue under the nails. Plenty of finger

prints all over the place, though. Only thing is, they were all hers and her husband's. They couldn't lift any prints off the rock. Too rough." He handed the file to Jackson. "It don't look good for your brother-in-law, Jackson."

Jackson took the folder. He was thinking the same thing. "Well, if he's guilty, he has to pay. Still, Sheriff, I don't think he did it. Hunch, or whatever. Mind if I do a little investigating?"

"Could I stop you?" Sheriff Gibbs drained the last of his coffee before he realized that it had gone cold. "Hey, Judge. Can I get you some coffee?"

Jackson nodded, and the other man disappeared through the door that led to the living quarters, leaving Jackson alone with Dooley, who, apparently satisfied with his nails, had dropped off to sleep, the toothpick drooping from the corner of his mouth.

Jackson's eye fell on the large conference table in the corner of the office. It was covered with rummage Norma Jean was saving for the church sale. He saw neat stacks of children's clothing, dishes, small appliances, and various other household items. Just as he had stepped over to get a closer look, the door opened and the sheriff came back, followed by Norma Jean carrying a tray with coffee and a plate of cookies.

"You didn't have to go to any trouble," Jackson said.

"No trouble. We don't get many visits from you, Judge." Norma Jean set the tray on the sheriff's desk, then stood beside Jackson. "I see you're admiring our merchandise."

"So that's what it is." Jackson grinned. "I was afraid it was evidence."

"I should be so lucky." The sheriff woke Dooley by knocking his feet off the desk. "Cream?"

Jackson shook his head. "Just black. Are you opening a store, Norma Jean?"

"Not on your life. This is donations for the church rummage sale and barbecue." She picked up a tiny baby gown and held it up. "Cute. Hey, Judge. I'll bet you and Patty have some stuff you could donate. Mind taking a look? It's for a good cause. All the proceeds will go to the children's home in Big Spring."

"I already did," Jackson said.

"Well, you be sure and come, now. This year's going to be special. The ladies decided to have a Harvest Festival along with the sale. There'll be craft booths and everything. We're all just so—"

Just then the phone rang and the sheriff scooped it up in his large hand. He listened for a moment, then said, "Where? Who's this? Okay, Walter, stay there. I'll be right out. And don't touch anything, you hear?" He put down the phone and looked at Jackson. "I've got to get out to Walter Pittman's place. There's been another murder."

TWENTY-TWO

LEONARD J. GIBBS HAD BEEN sheriff of Post Oak County for thirty years and hoped to retire after his birthday next year. In his profession, he'd seen plenty of bodies, those who fell victim to foul play, accident, or just plain old age. He had fished them out of the lake and sometimes had to scrape them off the highway. Once he'd had to cut down a man who'd hanged himself from a barn rafter. But never in his long career had he seen anything like this poor child. She lay naked except for one red sock in the brown-green pasture of the Pittman farm, one arm thrown over her face as if to ward off blows, the other, almost severed, stretched high above her head. Her unnaturally black hair, damp from the falling mist, hung lank across her face. A look of terror still lingered in the gray, dead eyes.

Jackson, who now wished he had declined to come along, felt Norma Jean Gibbs's cookies rising in his throat. He swallowed hard and forced himself to look again. No clothes scattered around the area, and no purse or shoes. Just this pathetic white body wearing one sock. She must have been about seventeen, Jackson thought, surely no older than that.

Dooley bent down for a closer look. "What's that thing around her neck? A necklace or something?"

"It's a tattoo." Jackson leaned in for a closer look. "My God, it's a hangman's noose."

"Kids nowadays got no respect for the bodies God gave 'um." Sheriff Gibbs shook his head. "Come on, Dooley, we got work to do."

The sheriff took a camera out of the back seat of his car and began photographing the scene, paying careful attention to the position of the body and the surrounding turf. While he was doing that, Dooley secured the area with yellow crime-scene tape. When he was satisfied, Sheriff Gibbs spoke briefly into his car radio, then walked over and stood beside Jackson. "The EMS will be here in a minute. I'm going to have a talk with Walter and his boy. See if they saw anything. You want to wait in the car?"

"I'd like to hear what they have to say."

Jackson followed the sheriff to where Pittman and his son stood huddled next to their shiny new John Deere. He'd known and liked Walter Pittman since he'd moved his family from Dallas and bought this farm. He wasn't much of a farmer, but didn't need to be. He had made a bundle from Nasdaq stocks and decided to retire to the country. They lived in a massive colonial house on a hill overlooking the ponds and pastures. Now Walter was pale and shaken.

The sheriff was wishing he had put the plastic cover over his Stetson before he left home. The rain pelted down harder. "Why don't we go up to the house to talk," he said. "Dooley can stay here and wait for the ambulance."

"Great idea!" Walter Pittman wanted to get as far away from there as possible.

When they entered the large paneled den, Pittman went immediately to the bar and offered drinks. The sheriff declined, saying he was on duty, but Jackson accepted gratefully.

When they were settled, Walter began his story without any prompting from the sheriff.

"Erin here was mowing the pasture—it hadn't started raining yet. He saw something white on the ground and thought a calf was down, so he went over to investigate. That's when he saw it was a body. He didn't touch a thing, just got on his cell phone and called the house. I came right out. That's all we know, Sheriff."

Sheriff Gibbs turned to the boy, who had disappeared into the kitchen and come back carrying a diet Coke. "That right, son?"

The boy looked at his shoes and nodded.

"Did you know the girl?"

"Of course he didn't know her." Walter Pittman's voice was smooth. "She must have been a transient or something."

"Erin?" The sheriff continued to address the boy.

Erin looked quickly at his father. "No, sir. I didn't know her."

"Right," the sheriff said. "Okay, that about does it. Oh, one other thing. I guess you heard about L. C. Warrick's goat."

"Lots of crazies around," Pittman said. "You see things like that all the time in the city. That's one reason I wanted to raise my kids in the country."

"No guarantees," the sheriff murmured. "So you haven't seen any strangers hanging around the area?"

"Absolutely not." Walter drained his drink and went to make another. "Judge?"

Jackson shook his head.

The sheriff rose. "Well, that about does it. You'll let us know if you think of anything?"

"Of course, Sheriff." Walter Pittman walked them to the door. At the door, he addressed Jackson. "How's old Ron holding up? He's been missing our regular Sunday round of golf."

"Well, you know, it's been a shock," Jackson answered. "I'll tell him you asked."

Thankfully, the rain had stopped. When they were back in the car, the sheriff turned to Jackson. "What's your take on it?"

"They could be hiding something."

"It's been my experience that most people are," the sheriff said as he turned the car around and headed back to town.

WILLIE NELSON ON the jukebox sang sorrowfully about the "night life" when Joe Bob Bonnet pushed open the door of Dad's Place on Highway 31 south of Post Oak. He stood for a moment inside the door, waiting for his eyes to become accustomed to the gloom before making his way toward the bar in the rear. The place was stifling due to the old-fashioned gas space heater standing against the wall, and smoke lay heavy in the air and mingled with the odors of unwashed bodies and stale beer. Joe Bob eased his ample rear onto a barstool and looked around him.

Hallie Whitiker, the owner of the place, was polishing glasses at the opposite end of the bar. He watched her thoughtfully. Almost six feet tall, she was rail-thin, with cherry-red hair arranged in a tall beehive and sprayed so lavishly with lacquer that the hair never moved even when she danced. Hallie wore skin-tight jeans with a Mexican concha belt. With it she wore a peasant blouse that revealed much of her scrawny chest and the barest hint of cleavage, which was painstakingly achieved by stuffing huge wads of cotton into the lower portion of her push-up bra. If she saw Joe Bob, she gave no evidence of it. Joe Bob slammed his fist on the bar, rattling the empty beer bottles lined in front of two farmhands at the far end. Hallie looked around as if she had just that minute noticed him.

"Oh, hey, Joe Bob. How long you been settin' there?"

"You know what I want." His voice was a growl.

"Oh, yeah. The usual, right?"

Joe Bob didn't answer. He had turned on his stool and was scanning the crowd.

Hallie poured a generous amount of whiskey in a shot glass, then drew a draft beer into a frosted mug. She set them in front of him. "Here you go."

He turned slowly and caught her eye. She looked away, then back at him. "What?"

He drained the shot and then the beer, pushing the glasses toward her. She quickly refilled them and shoved them toward him. "What?"

"Where's she at?"

"Who? Renita? She's in back, Joe Bob. In her room. When did you get back to town?"

"Last night. Go get her."

"I cain't, Job Bob," she whined. You go on back there and you can see her. She's in her room. Ain't nobody with her."

"I want to dance."

"Oh, well, if that's all you want, I'll dance with you. I'm not too busy. Or, looky there. There's some ladies over by the jukebox that look like they're just dyin' to dance."

Joe Bob did not look at the women; he stared instead at Hallie. "Get her."

Hallie rebelled. "I ain't. You want to get me closed down? The liquor boys will do that quicker'n you can spit if they catch her in here. She ain't but fifteen." She spoke rapidly, not looking at him. "I got real problems with that girl. Now the school's after me because she ain't been going. I told them I was home-schooling her, but I don't think they bought it. Truth is, Joe Bob, I couldn't make it here without the little bit I can make off her— Hey, ouch! That hurts."

Joe Bob, leaning over the bar, twisted her wrist until she screamed with pain. "Okay, I'm goin'. Let go now. I mean it—you're gonna break it!"

Slowly, he released her and she turned and walked the length of the bar and down a short hallway under a sign marked *Restrooms*. He heard a door open. "Renita! Renita Rae, get out here."

While he waited, Joe Bob downed the shot and started on the beer, drinking more slowly this time.

Hallie returned. "She'll be out in a minute. She's fixing her face. You want another?"

He nodded and she refilled the shot glass.

"Beer, too?"

He shook his head, never taking his eyes off the passageway that led to the restrooms. In a moment she came, tiny and thin, with mouse-colored hair that hung straight around her heart-shaped face. Her ears protruded through the hair. She, like her mother, wore tight jeans. Hints of developing breasts made molehills on the yellow tank top she wore. She looked at the floor as she approached him. "Hey, Joe Bob."

Her took her arm and led her to a table in the darkest corner of the room. "You been good?" he asked after they were seated.

"Uh-huh." She looked at the ceiling.

"You ain't got a boyfriend since I left, have you?"

"Who, me? No."

"Shit, I believe you. Who'd want a little hooker like you?" Grinning, he got up and put coins in the jukebox, then returned and stood beside her. "Come on, let's dance a little before we go on back. It makes me horny—and you know how you like it when I get horny, don'tcha, honey?" He cupped his hand around her buttocks as he followed her to the dance floor.

TWENTY-THREE

A BRIGHT BLUE SKY and a cool breeze made for the perfect day as Jackson pulled his car into a parking spot a block from the church. He opened the car door and held it for Mandy to get out.

"Mind walking across the park?"

"Love to," she said.

From the top of the hill where they stood, the park lay drowsing in the sunlight. Drifts of fallen leaves made mounds around the metal swings, slides, and teeter-totters, overflowed the sandboxes and barbecue pits, and floated like tiny boats in the fishpond. Squirrels rummaged happily in the leaves, filling their cheeks with pecans for the winter and chattering fussily at the intruders. Noisy blue jays squawked overhead as if they owned the place. Jackson took Mandy's hand in his as they walked through the park and made their way toward the churchyard where the Harvest Festival and rummage sale were being presented by the ladies of First Baptist. The women had decided this year to hold the affair on the green lawn between the Fellowship Hall and the sanctuary. Before the church had bought the lot next door, the sale took place in the basement of the century-old church building. The structure had been modernized after the

Fellowship Hall was built, so now the front of the
church consisted of two solid brick walls, joined in
the middle at a forty-five-degree angle where the
walls rose sharply heavenward. This gave the appearance of the prow of a ship. The rear had been left
alone and still retained its gothic details and stained-
glass windows. A few older members of the congregation thought it was a shame to change it, but the
majority applauded its clean lines and bare simplicity.
Like Christ, they said. Baptists had never gone in for
popish ornamentation. A simple building for a simple
faith.

Jackson was glad Mandy had agreed to join him
for the day. They could look at the exhibits, eat barbecue, and later drive out to the country club for
drinks. She wore a red sundress with white trim,
which set off her honey-colored skin nicely, Jackson
thought.

They strolled through the crafts display in the covered walkway that separated the hall from the sanctuary. Jane Archer presided over the area with the zeal
of a Midway barker.

"How-do, Judge and Miz Dee-Alendro."

"Call me Mandy. Everybody does." Mandy smiled
at the way the woman mangled her name.

"Sure will! Judge, come on over here. I want to
show you these big ashtrays Alice Hull made in ce-
ramics. They'd go perfect in your office for those ci-
gars you smoke."

Jackson studied the ashtrays and made appropriate
comments, although he doubted that naked ladies, no
matter how tastefully done, would be suitable for his

office at the courthouse. He grinned. "Has Brother Steve seen these?"

Jane picked up one of the pieces and examined it. "He did, and he tried to say something, but then Alice explained to him that they were copied right out of a book of classical Grecian figures." She put the piece down. "I still don't think he liked them too much. But when Alice reminded him it was to make money for the orphans, he just shook his head and walked away."

Muriel, with two young boys in tow, waited in line for pony rides. Jackson introduced her to Mandy. Muriel, far too subtle to say anything, smiled at Jackson to let him know she was glad he had followed her advice and asked Mandy out.

"Who are your friends here?" Jackson asked.

"Oh, this is Jeramy and this is Josh. They're my sister's kids." She poked the boys, who were poking twigs into cone-shaped doodlebug holes in the sandy ground. "Say hi to the judge and Mandy, boys."

The boys got to their feet and dutifully spoke. "We goin' to ride them ponies," Josh said.

"I bet you'll be scared," Jeramy said, poking his brother with his finger.

"I ain't. Aunt Muriel, tell him I ain't scared. I ain't one bit scared of any old pony."

Jackson pulled a bill out of his pocket. "In that case, I guess you'd both better ride twice," he said.

"Fall days always remind me of school," Mandy said as they walked away from Muriel and the boys.

"Me, too. Football games, hayrides, Halloween."

Jackson took her elbow and guided her to a bench under a tree.

"I guess everybody has the same memories of high school—no matter where you grew up. In south Texas, we didn't have very pronounced seasons, not like up here. But there was always a day or two when you could just feel the fall in the air—then it got hot again." She laughed.

Jackson was so taken by the sound of her voice that he almost forgot to answer. Then he caught himself. "Like something to drink?"

They made their way back through the crowd to the drink stand, which was set up against the brick wall of the building. It was a hastily constructed cube, with bare planks set chest-high serving as a bar. Red and yellow beach umbrellas served as shade. Edna Buchannan presided. Patty and her friends were leaning against one board counter drinking Cokes. Patty urged the little gang to leave the minute she saw Jackson and Mandy coming their way. Jackson grinned as he spotted Sonny Smart sticking close to Patty's side.

"Hell's bells, Jackson, I wish you'd look over there." Edna pointed toward the used clothing tables. "There's those Rices, pawing through the stuff. Don't they know that's for the poor people?"

"Two lemonades." Jackson was hoping to avoid the issue.

Edna addressed Mandy. "See those old farts? They're the richest folks in town. You'd never know it, though. They live like paupers on account of him being so stingy." She filled two plastic cups with shaved ice and poured lemonade out of a glass jar. "Here you go. That'll be one dollar even."

The long paper-covered eating tables had been decorated by Vanessa Largent. There had been a certain amount of comment concerning the decorations. The women thought the blue spatterware pitchers filled with red geraniums and twined with English ivy added a lot to the ambience of the meal. Most of the men declared they got in the way of talking to your neighbor across the way. Jackson and Mandy took seats next to Sheriff Gibbs and his wife, Norma Jean.

Naturally, everybody wanted to know all about the murder out at Walter Pittman's place. The sheriff made a face. "I'm not allowed to talk about it. Right, Judge?"

Jackson nodded. He was sure he didn't want to talk about it. "Good ribs," he commented, hoping to direct the conversation elsewhere.

"The best," Mrs. Gibbs said, and reached for another to show she meant it.

Just then, Mae Applewaite rushed up. She was holding a Red Lion plastic grocery bag, tied at the top. She plopped it down on the table. "Sheriff, I want you to see what somebody left on our clothing table. It's disgusting!"

The sheriff took the bag and opened it. He took out a pair of very small and very soiled black jeans, a black T-shirt, and a pair of worn and dirty running shoes. The last thing to come out was one red sock.

"Where did this come from?" he demanded.

"I just told you. Some fool left it on our clothing table. The idea!"

The sheriff put the things back into the bag and set it on the bench beside him. "Watch this, will you, Judge?" He stood up. "I'm going to wash my hands."

Jackson addressed Mae. "Did anyone see who left it there?"

"No, Judge, I told you, it just appeared. One of those wild Lutheran kids, is what I'm thinking. Come over here to sabotage our sale!"

TWENTY-FOUR

JACKSON AND MANDY strolled through the lobby of the country club. They stopped at the desk so Jackson could introduce Mandy to club manager Sam Profit and Sam's golden retriever, Lady. Sam had had polio as a child and used a wheelchair. Lady, his helper dog, thumped her tail in greeting. She wore a sign saying: *Please Do Not Pet Me.*

"Anybody in the club tonight?" Jackson asked.

"Just the regulars. Everybody's over at the barbecue." Sam grinned. "Fine with me. I can use the peace and quiet."

Mandy hid a smile when they entered the club.

Esther Franklin had taken on the job of decorating the clubhouse. She felt responsible, she said, because her husband, Everett, an avid golfer, had donated the sixty acres the club was built on. Everett had come from old money. His ancestor was one of the founders of Post Oak County, and no one was surprised when his mother kicked up a real stink when Everett got Esther pregnant and had to marry her. The reason for the stink was that Esther's father worked at the feed mill and her mother cooked at the high school cafeteria. In spite of different backgrounds, as far as anybody could tell, the marriage had been a success. Esther took to riches like a duck to water and was soon hoarding money like a pro. Old Mrs. Franklin had finally relented and now insisted she'd never objected to the marriage in the first place.

Every room in the clubhouse had a theme. The large dining room was English manor house while the small lunchroom was done up as a French bistro. The ladies' lounge emulated a country garden with lots of latticework and flowery chintz. The room that Jackson and Mandy now entered was decorated with a golf motif. The mirror behind the bar was framed with gold golf trophies, and the handles on all the taps were golf balls. Grass-green plush carpeting covered the floor. Golf bags and clubs of every age and description hung on the paneled walls along with Esther's own paintings of the golf course. In a place of honor near the entrance stood a life-sized mannequin dressed in replicas of the plus fours, cap, and shoes the great Ben Hogan himself had worn.

Jackson and Mandy found two armchairs near a pair of French doors overlooking the golf course. They ordered drinks. Jackson had scotch; Mandy decided on a frozen margarita.

Mandy took a sip of her drink and smiled. "Umm, good." She set the drink down. "Now talk to me."

"What?"

"You know, tell me about yourself. Seems like I've told you my life story, and I don't know much at all about you." She crossed her arms and waited for him to start.

As far as Jackson could see, she'd talked mostly about the Main Street Program and precious little about herself, but he wasn't one to split hairs. "Not much to tell," he said. "I was born right here in Post Oak. My dad was a judge and my mom was active in civic work. I went through all twelve years of school here. After graduation I went to UT Austin for my bachelor's degree and later got my law license there. Got out in '72 and came back here. End of story."

"I doubt that." Mandy stretched and crossed her ankles. "Who were your friends in school? Where did you meet your wife?" She ducked her head. "Oh, gosh. I guess I'm really being nosy. Forget I asked."

Jackson laughed. "You look like a little girl that's been caught poking through her mother's purse. I have no secrets. Let's see, now. You've probably met a lot of the people I grew up with. Muriel—remember her from the Wagon Wheel? Well, we went all the way through school together. And Horace Kincaid down at the newspaper, he was the quarterback on our football team, the Panthers. Fastest runner in three counties. Horace married Margie Law, who was my girlfriend in ninth grade. Sheriff Gibbs is a native, too. He's a good bit older than me, but his wife, Norma Jean, was just one grade ahead of me." Jackson paused and inhaled. "Sounds kind of inbred, doesn't it? But it's not that way. A lot of new people have come to town, and we've welcomed most of them."

"Tell me about Gretchen."

Jackson tried to remember whether he'd ever told her Gretchen's name. "She grew up in Dallas. I met her when I was at the university in Austin. She was the prettiest girl I'd ever seen and the sweetest. We married right out of college and came here to live. She was a good wife and mother. She was too young to die. What else can I say?''

''No more than you want to, and I didn't mean to pry.'' She drained her drink. ''I should get home.''

Jackson looked at his watch. ''You're right, it's getting late.''

When they got back to Mandy's apartment, Jackson got out of the car and held the door while she got out. Mandy laughed softly as he escorted her up the front steps.

''What's funny?''

''Nothing. It's just that I haven't had too many men walk me to the door lately. Mostly they just let you out at the curb. If they're polite, they wait in the car until you're safely inside.''

Jackson feigned a frown. ''Does that mean I'm quaint?''

''Maybe.'' She leaned toward him. ''Would you like to kiss me good-night?''

Jackson took her in his arms. Her lips were pliant and sweet, and the kiss lasted longer than he'd planned. When he finally let her go, his heart was pounding. He touched her cheek and reluctantly turned away.

As he started the car, he turned for one last look at the house. She was standing at the window waving. Jackson Crain smiled broadly all the way home.

SHERIFF GIBBS STARED morosely at the mess on his desk. Its worn oak top was hidden under a mountain of files and another mountain of loose papers waiting to be filed. Certainly he had no time to do it, not with two murders on his hands and, for the last two days, the Rangers working out of his office. The commissioners were just going to have to spring for a secretary for him. He would put it to them at their next meeting.

The phone rang—again. It had been ringing off the wall since the last murder. He'd already given interviews to the three television stations in the area, and this morning a reporter from Channel Four in Dallas had called. The sheriff let the answering machine pick up but listened to the message. It was Horace Kinkaid wanting to know the latest. Well, Horace would have to wait.

Sheriff Gibbs picked up the phone and called Jackson Crain. In five minutes, Jackson was seated in the chair opposite his desk.

"I thought you'd want to see this." The sheriff pointed to the table where, a few days before, the rummage-sale things were stored. Now all it held was a dirty khaki backpack.

Jackson walked over for a closer look. "What's this?"

"Rangers found it not thirty yards from the body." Leonard Gibbs handed Jackson a pair of latex gloves. "Open it up."

Jackson pulled on the gloves, then unzipped the backpack and drew out a pair of minuscule army fatigue pants and a dirty white T-shirt. He reached in again and this time withdrew a handkerchief-sized piece of silk, which revealed itself to be a pair of panties. He quickly dropped the item. "The victim's." He looked at the sheriff. "That all?"

"Only this." Sheriff Gibbs unzipped the side pocket and withdrew what appeared to be a small leather book. When he opened it, Jackson saw it was a double picture frame. Inside was a photo of a teenage girl sitting on a beach and holding a baby in her lap. On the facing side where another photograph should have been was a slip of paper that bore the inscription, *Bougainvillea and Dorothea, Rockport, 1985.* "What I'm thinking is, that baby could be our victim. She would have been a baby around '85. But Jackson, I want you to look at the other girl. Don't she look familiar to you?"

Jackson looked hard at the picture. "No. Can't say she does. Mind if I take it out of the frame?

The sheriff nodded. "Go ahead."

Jackson removed the photo and walked to the window. "There's something...maybe the eyes. I don't know. Who do you think she looks like?"

"That's just it, Jackson. I can't get a handle on it. But there's something about that face that reminds me of someone in this town, and damned if I can figure out who it is."

"Well, maybe it'll come to you. Anything else?"

"Matter of fact, there is. When they got her over to the funeral home to clean her up, the medical examiner staff found another tattoo behind her right shoulder. It was a snake coiled in the shape of a heart. Is that sick, or what? And inside the heart were the words *'Boogie and Mick Forever.'* Judge, I'm thinking Boogie might just be a nickname for Bougainvillae.''

"Sounds right." Jackson slipped the photo back inside the frame. "Anything official on her?"

Leonard Gibbs sat back down and took a sip from the coffee mug on his desk. "Lord, that stuff's ice-cold. You want a Coke, Judge?"

Jackson nodded. The sheriff disappeared through the door that divided his office from his living quarters and returned carrying two canned sodas. "Diet or regular?"

Jackson shrugged and Gibbs handed him the diet cola. Jackson repeated his question. "Any ID on her?"

"Nope. No driver's license or any other identifying papers. I've e-mailed Austin for a missing persons report. They haven't responded yet. Maybe her family's looking for her—maybe not. A lot of these kids, Judge, are just throwaways. It's either they've got no family or their families just don't give a damn. It's sad, is what it is."

Jackson shook his head, thinking of Patty.

Back in his office, Jackson found Edna sitting at his desk. She was reading a letter. "Jackson." She waved the letter at him. "This came in today's mail. It's from TxDOT. They want you to come down and meet with them next week."

"Let's see." Jackson took the letter from the Texas Department of Transportation and sat down on one of the two leather client's chairs. After he'd read it, he spoke. "Okay. Clear my schedule for Monday and

Tuesday—better make it three days in case I get tied up.''

''Jackson, you tell them the folks at Willow Creek get stranded every rainy season when the creek rises. Those folks need that new road with a decent bridge. Remember two years ago? Lissa Peters had her baby with nobody but her mama and her husband helping her because they couldn't get in to the hospital. Tell them about that, too.''

''I will,'' Jackson said. ''Anything else going on?''

''Nope.''

''Then I'm going home. You know where to find me if you need to.''

''Get out of here. I wish you would. Shit, go fishing or something. Call up that little Main Street lady and take her with you. You've been nothing but a work-aholic ever since Gretchen died.''

Jackson walked home thinking he might just call up Mandy, but fishing was definitely the last thing on his mind.

TWENTY-FIVE

A COOL BREEZE CARESSED Vanessa's face. She tilted her head backward and watched two sparrows fussing over the bird feeder hanging from the mulberry tree. In summer, the feeder had harbored a multitude of birds of all kinds, but now only the sparrows, jays, and a few blackbirds remained. Vanessa was content to feed them through the winter even though most people considered them nuisances. She stretched and shifted to a more comfortable position in the old metal lawn chair. It was Sunday evening and she and Steve were enjoying the last of the balmy fall days. Steve lay back with his eyes closed while she amused herself watching the birds.

Finally, she spoke. "Honey..."

Steve looked at her. "Yes, love?"

"You haven't called me that in a long time."

"I haven't? Funny, I always think of you that way."

"Do you really? I'm glad. Sometimes I think you'd like to trade me in on a new model. You know, go down to the wife dealership and look over their stock. Maybe they'd be running a special on preacher's wives."

"You're a nut. Know that?"

"I guess. Steve…"

"What?"

"Why haven't we had a child?"

"Vanessa, you know we've talked about this."

"I know, it's just that I'm going to be thirty-three in December. My clock's ticking, honey. Do you want kids? Honestly?"

Steve put down the paper and took her hand, turning to look her in the eye. "Van, I want children with you. I want a little girl with red hair and a free spirit. I want her to be just like you." His eyes held hers. "Do you believe I mean that?"

Vanessa nodded.

"But I don't want to bring a child into this house. You're not happy here and, face it, we just don't have the room. I wasn't going to mention this, but maybe now's the time. Honey, I've heard from First Baptist in Graystone. They're looking to call a new preacher, and they want me to come and preach a revival the first week in January. If they like me, it'll be a big step forward. That church had over a thousand members, Van."

"You mean you'd leave Post Oak?"

"Of course, honey. A career in the ministry is just like any other career. You have to move up to better yourself. Congregations and pastors need the change, otherwise both will go stagnant, and the Lord doesn't want that. We're called, just like St. Paul, to minister in many places."

"Then you wouldn't mind if we had a baby later, if you get the job?"

"Not only would I not mind, I'd be proud and happy."

Vanessa thought about it. "I'd miss Post Oak, though."

"Would you? Really?"

"I think I would. I've made a new friend, you know. Mandy de Alejandro."

"Well, I wouldn't worry yet. It's not a done deal." He frowned. "We may be staying here another year or two."

Vanessa watched as a harvest moon, orange as a pumpkin, peeped over the oleander hedge. "Steve?"

"Um-hum?"

"Do you love what you're doing—I mean, really love it?"

He swallowed hard. "Truthfully, Van, I'm having a hard time right now. Don't get me wrong, my conversion was real. I know without a doubt that I'm meant to serve. It's just that…I don't know…it's the administrative stuff. And paperwork—I hate the paperwork!"

"I guess that goes with it."

"I guess, but it's not just that. It's the politics of it all. Everybody's got their own ideas about how the church should be run. Sometimes it's not much different from the military."

Vanessa's eyes widened. "Really? Why haven't we discussed this before?"

"I think I just this minute realized it myself." He rushed on. "Van, what I wanted to do was help people. Now, when I hear all the bickering and gossip in the church—"

Vanessa broke in. "Suppose there was another way to serve God. Would you be willing to consider it even if it meant leaving the ministry?"

"Lord, Van! Leave the ministry?"

"Sure. If you found another way of helping people, what difference would it make?"

"I don't know, honey. I honestly don't know. Anyway, what would I do?"

"Pray about it," she said. "Maybe the answer will come."

He squeezed her hand. "You're right, I will."

PATTY PEDDLED her bicycle up Hill Avenue to her friend Bitsy's house. Her legs felt heavy; in fact, her whole body felt heavy. Perspiration ran down her neck and between her shoulder blades. She wondered if she wasn't getting too old to ride a bike everywhere she went. She thought briefly about how free she had felt last summer, flying all over town on her bicycle, not feeling tired or self-conscious the way she sometimes did now. The whole of last summer had passed in a blur of swimming parties, picnics, and lazy afternoons sitting in the swing drinking Cokes and reading—or playing Monopoly at friends' houses, never once wondering if her hair looked right or if she looked fat in her swimsuit. Now she was in eighth grade and everything had changed. Lately it seemed all she and her friends talked about was boys. And a new word had insinuated itself into the girls' vocabularies. The word was "popular."

Patty saw Sonny Smart riding toward her. Oh, great. That's all I need, she thought. Pretending she didn't see him, she quickly turned into Miss Mabel Skidmore's driveway. She hid herself and her bike in Miss Mabel's rose garden until he passed the house, riding slow and looking hard, trying to see where she'd gone.

That was another thing she couldn't figure out, Sonny Smart. They'd been friends since kindergarten, a free and easy friendship that had been blind to gender differences. Lately, she had begun to notice things about him she couldn't believe she'd overlooked. For instance, his ears didn't match; one was larger and closer to his head than the other. Not only that, one of the ears, the one that stuck out more, had a large wart right on its tip. And he had practically no eyelashes at all. She peeked around the corner of the house to make sure Sonny was gone, then mounted her bike and rode on to Bitsy's house.

Bitsy greeted Patty at the door wearing a tank top and shorts. "C'mon in. Want a Coke or something?"

Patty nodded and followed Bitsy into the kitchen. "What are you doing?"

"Nothing much." Bitsy took a can of Coke out of the refrigerator. "I was listening to my new CD. Want to hear it?"

Later, sprawled on Bitsy's bed listening to the music, Bitsy said, "Hey, I hear your dad's got a girl-friend. Ga-ross!"

"No way! Who told you that?"

"Heard my mom and them talking. They said it's the Mexican woman that's running the Main Street thingy."

Patty sat up cross-legged on the bed. "The way

people talk in this town. He's, like, just being nice to her because she's new in town. My dad's not interested in anything but me and his job. He told me so a long time ago—right after Mama died.''

"Well, things can change, can't they? I wonder if they kiss." Bitsy giggled. "I bet they French-kiss."

"You are so disgusting!"

"I get he gives her the tongue every time they kiss each other." Bitsy fell over on the bed, shaking with laughter.

"You're hateful and I'm going home!"

Bitsy followed her to the door, still laughing. "Wait, Pats, don't go. I was just kidding. Come on back up…" But the door had already slammed behind her friend.

It was almost dark when Patty peddled into her own yard, angry tears stinging her eyes. She dropped her bike beside the back steps and ran up to her room, never noticing the privet hedge that separated the back yard from the alley shifting slightly, or the eyes that watched until the light came on in her room.

TWENTY-SIX

MANDY DE ALEJANDRO looked at the tallow tree that grew outside her office window. Now it was covered with the tiny white fruit that hung from its twigs in pairs like cherries, and its heart-shaped leaves were golden against the blue sky. Suddenly she realized that the room had grown silent and the man across her desk was looking at her questioningly.

"What? I'm afraid I was..."

"Woolgathering?" Morgan Smith grinned. "I was just saying, the Main Street Program ought to extend the new sidewalks another block, is all. Be the best thing for all concerned, is my way of thinking."

Morgan owned an auto parts store across the railroad tracks from the main row of stores that constituted Post Oak's business district.

Mandy nodded. "I see your point. The only thing is, Mr. Smith..."

Mandy looked especially pretty today dressed in an apple green skirt with a frilly blouse of a creamy silk material. Jade earrings shaped like hearts swung from her ears. "Call me Morgan."

"...Morgan, yours is the only business on that block since the movie theater burned down. Don't most people drive up to your store?"

"I reckon they do at that. Still and all, them brick sidewalks and maybe a tub of flowers out front would sure beautify the town. Ain't that what you're here for?"

"There are budget considerations—and it would have to go before the committee, you know."

Morgan pushed back his chair and got to his feet. "That's all I'm asking, ma'am. Just give it some thought. I won't take any more of your time today."

Mandy stood and offered her hand. "Thank you for coming in Mr....Morgan. Why don't you check with me sometime next week."

When he had left, Mandy delved into the mound of paperwork on her desk. By the time she had closed the last file and added it to the neat stack waiting to be stored away, it was noon. Normally, Mandy brought a sandwich from home for her lunch. Some days, she would walk the short distance from the office to her little rent house and have her lunch there. Today, she decided to stroll downtown and have a salad at the Wagon Wheel. She picked up her purse and left the building, locking the door behind her.

The short walk to the café was uneventful. She passed the large Victorian home next door, which had been recently purchased by a group of attorneys and converted to offices. The massive magnolia tree in front grew over the sidewalk, with its branches almost sweeping the ground. A mockingbird swooped down from its depths, its squawks warning her to stay away. Mandy smiled and continued to the corner, where she turned right as she passed the Dollar Store. At the antique mall, she met Mae Applewaite.

"Morning, Mandy." Mae bustled up to her. "Don't see you out and about much. They keeping you busy?"

Mandy smiled and nodded. "I'm just going over to the Wagon Wheel for lunch."

"That old greasy spoon." Mae made a face. "Honey, you ought to try the sandwich shop Puddy Hawkes opened up. Have you been there yet?"

"Good idea," Mandy agreed. "I wasn't sure whether they had opened the doors yet. Will you join me?"

"Sure will." Mae fell into step beside Mandy. "I was just going down to the Knitter's Nook anyway and it's right across the street."

"I've heard Puddy is a very good cook."

"The best," Mae agreed. "Now, you tell everybody you see about her place. It's hard for new businesses to get going in this town, what with people being so awfully set in their ways."

"I will," Mandy said pushing open the door that led into the narrow building. "My, this is very nice."

The black and white floor tiles had been scrubbed and waxed to a bright shine and in a row down the center of the room stood four tables covered in green-and-white-checked tablecloths, each bearing a copper bowl filled with fresh marigolds. Green and white café curtains hung in the window. Puddy, plump and rosy and wearing a frilly apron, trotted over to greet them.

"Come on in," she said. "You're my first customers of the day." She escorted them to a table. "Our specials for the day are shrimp quiche and pasta primavera.''

Mae ordered the pasta and Mandy settled for a garden salad. When Puddy had brought out their orders accompanied by a basket of hot homemade rolls, Mae leaned toward Mandy.

''You heard all about the second murder, I guess?''

Mandy buttered a roll and nodded.

Mae had heard the story on more than one occasion. Now she proceeded to tell Mandy her version, taking delicate bites of pasta as she talked and waving her fork for emphasis.

''What happened was, they found her out at Walt Pittman's place. Walt's boy found her. You know them?''

Mandy shook her head.

''New folks. Moved here from Dallas. They say he's got money. Anyway, as it happened, Jackson was in talking to the sheriff when the call came in. He rode out there with the sheriff and Dooley. Dooley's the one told me. He said it was just awful. She was just a kid. Did you know that?''

''I heard,'' Mandy said.

''Dooley said her arm was mighty near ripped off…and her head was bashed in. She might have been strangled and raped, too. They won't know until they get the medical report, he says.''

''Isn't this a lovely day?'' Mandy said, hoping to change the subject.

''What? Oh, yeah, lovely.'' She raised her voice. ''Puddy, do you suppose we could have a few more rolls over here?''

After Puddy had seated a group of women newly arrived, she brought the rolls. "I sure would like to have the recipe for these," Mae said.

Puddy winked. "Professional secret."

"I could probably figure it out, if I wanted to," Mae confided to Mandy. "Anyway, about the murder. I ran into Norma Jean Gibbs at the Piggly Wiggly and *she* said the girl had tattoos on her. I mean big ones. One going all around her neck in the shape of a rope. Isn't that something?"

Mandy's mind had wandered. "What? I'm sorry."

"The tattoo…a rope around her neck. Anyway, do you remember that bag somebody left at the rummage sale? With the nasty clothes in it?"

Mandy finished her salad and took a sip of tea. "Yes."

"Well, later they found her backpack. And would you believe it, they found a photo in there. It was of a woman and a baby—and on the back it said Bougainvillea and Frankie. Sheriff says he figures maybe Bougainvillea was the girl's name because she had 'Boogie' tattooed on…wait!…where are you going?"

Mandy had tossed some bills on the table and was hurrying toward the door. "Just remembered," she said over her shoulder. "I have an appointment."

Mae stared openmouthed as Mandy disappeared down the sidewalk. "Well, doesn't that just beat all," she said to no one in particular.

Jackson was looking out the window of his office and saw Mandy hurrying past the courthouse. He sprinted down the stairs to say hello to her, but she had already disappeared into the sheriff's office before he reached the ground floor.

VANESSA WAS A GOOD COOK. In her mind that was a lot more important than housekeeping, and if he was honest with himself, she was sure Steve would agree. Now she took a rack of lamb crusted with mustard and seasoned ground walnuts out of the oven. It smelled heavenly. While it rested on the counter, she began stringing the snow peas, which, along with tiny new potatoes, she would serve with the lamb. She was making this special meal to cheer him up. Steve had seemed down in the dumps since they had talked the other night about his job.

She had just put the vegetables into the steamer when Steve entered the combination kitchen and family room. After kissing her, he dropped his briefcase on the table and sank into his favorite chair with a sigh.

Vanessa came and sat on the ottoman at his feet. "Tough day?"

Steve caressed her hair. "The toughest, hon. It's budget time, and the deacons want me to preach on tithing this Sunday. You know how I feel...."

"I do, sweet. And I agree. People shouldn't have to be harangued about money when they come to church. Stand up for yourself!"

"It's not that easy, I'm afraid. The church has to have money to pay for the new building—plus the regular cost of running things. The air-conditioning is on its last legs. If that compressor goes out..."

"I know. Fifteen thousand. You told me. So, are you going to? Preach on tithing, I mean?"

Steve got up and removed his coat, hanging it on the back of a kitchen chair. He walked over to the stove and peeked at the steaming vegetables. "Smells great. I guess I'll have to." He sank back into his chair. "But that's not going to solve the problem. Even if every member of the congregation gave ten percent, we still wouldn't have enough. Now the deacons are talking about a membership drive. You know, organizing the congregation into teams and canvassing the town for new members." Vanessa made a face. Steve continued. "Another avenue is to have a revival—get a big-name preacher to come in and hold it, special music, the works."

Vanessa looked at Steve but didn't respond.

"You don't like any of this, do you?"

Vanessa spoke carefully. "You know how I feel, Steve. First of all, there are no more Baptists in this town. What are you going to do, raid the Methodists and Presbyterians? Convert some Catholics or Lutherans? Come on!"

"You just don't understand, Van." He got up, walked to the French doors, and looked out into the back yard for a long time. "This is not what you imagined when we married. A suburban back yard, the neighbors' houses smack up against you." He turned to face her. "Is it?"

Vanessa shook her head.

He came back and stood over her. "Did I do the wrong thing, Van? All I wanted to do was serve the Lord. Now I wonder if I could have served Him better on a farm with you, maybe with children—if not our own, then foster children like that poor kid they found murdered. Me writing and you painting. I just don't know, Van.''

Vanessa nodded, then stood up and went to the stove. "Go and change," she said. "You'll feel better after you eat. Later, I'll give you a back rub.''

TWENTY-SEVEN

JACKSON AND HORACE Kinkaid took seats in their favorite booth near the back at the Wagon Wheel. The usual morning coffee crowd was there. Edna Buchannan sat at a table up front with three of the girls from the title company, while the Haygood brothers hunched over the counter flanking Reginald Hopkins, the town's oldest living bachelor. Several matrons taking a break from the morning's shopping sipped coffee and munched donuts at a table by the window.

Rip came and stood by their table.

Horace looked at the dark circles under Rip's eyes. "You look like a raccoon with a hangover."

"Eat shit," Rip said.

"You got any? It might be an improvement over that mess you passed off as stew last week." Horace winked at Jackson.

"Y'all want coffee, or do you just want to set here and run off at the mouth all day?"

"Coffee," Jackson said.

"I'll have decaf." Horace made a face. "It tastes like horse piss, but Doc says it's either that or fall over dead with a stroke."

Rip left and came back with the coffee. He nudged Horace over and sat down in the booth next to him.

"I ain't stopped since six o'clock this morning," he said.

"Why? Where's Muriel?" Jackson couldn't remember ever coming in for morning coffee and not seeing Muriel, except the time she had her appendix out and Edna's daughter, Pammy, came in to help out for a week.

"Well, hell, Rip. Aren't you worried? This is not like Muriel, is it?" Horace took a sip of coffee and made a face.

"Haven't had time to be worried." Rip frowned. "You know, now I think of it, she ain't never done this before that I can recollect."

"Did she seem okay when she left last night?"

Rip's eyes widened. "Oh, shit. I must be getting all-timer's disease. She left last night with that brother-in-law of yours, Jackson. And that ain't all. I saw Joe Bob driving down the street right after they left."

Jackson drew in a breath. "The husband? Do you think he was following them?"

"Don't know. I went on out back and started cleaning up." Rip stood up. "I'm gonna call her right now."

"Bring some more coffee before you do," Horace said. "And this time, I'll take the real stuff. To hell with doctors anyway."

Rip brought the coffee, then disappeared into the little office off the dining room.

Edna walked up. "I'm going back to the office, Jackson—and you better get there pretty soon. We've got to get a letter off to Austin before the mail goes out.''

"Right. Be there in ten minutes.''

"How come you're writing Austin?'' Horace never forgot he was a reporter.

"It's about the new road. Austin turned down our request—but there's still a chance. We're getting some of the folks out at Willow Creek to sign a petition, then I'm going to hand-carry it to the highway department.''

"When do you reckon you might be going?'' Horace pressed for more news.

"Maybe as early as next week. The petition is circulating now. Why? You want to go with me?''

"Me?'' Horace's sandy eyebrows knitted together. "Hmm. I might could. Do you want company?''

"Sure.''

"Then let me talk to the old lady and—''

Rip came back to the table pale as a corpse. "She's been beat up.'' He eased himself back into the booth. "Jackson, y'all got to go see about her. I can't leave. The lunch crowd's already starting to come in.'' Rip's voice trembled. "Please, Jackson.''

"Don't you think we ought to call the EMS?''

"She wouldn't let me. Said she was okay. But she sounded awful, Jackson.''

"Did you tell her somebody would be there to check on her?''

"Yeah. You know where she lives? Over on Redbud Street—little blue house on the corner.''

Jackson looked around the room for a woman to go along, but Edna had already left and the matron shoppers probably didn't even know Muriel's name. What the hell, he and Horace could at least go and look in on her. If she was badly hurt, they could call an ambulance the same as a woman could.

They left the café and got into Horace's maroon Toyota. Redbud Street ran east and west on the south side of town past the railroad tracks. The houses along both sides of the street were small, some covered with composition siding manufactured to simulate brick and mortar, others particolored for want of a paint job or weathered gray from never having been painted at all. Children played ball in a vacant lot using flat sandstone rocks for bases, while others, hollering like whooping cranes, chased each other down the middle of the street on ancient bikes. There were no side-walks. Bass boats and cars on blocks decorated front yards and gravel driveways. Horace parked the car in front of a house with blue vinyl siding. Concrete urns on either side of the doorstep spilled over with bronze chrysanthemums. The sprinkler must have been run-ning all night. The yard was a lake and the water poured down the driveway and into the street. Jackson knocked on the door, while Horace sloshed across the yard to turn off the water.

When no one came to the door, Jackson knocked again, louder this time. "You stay here," he said to Horace. "I'll go around back."

Jackson walked around the side of the little house, noting that the blinds were tightly closed. In back, a flight of concrete steps led to a small screened porch. Jackson tried the screen door. It scraped against the wooden floor as he pushed it open. He looked through the glass window of the kitchen door, then quickly picked up an empty flowerpot, broke the glass, and reached inside to turn the doorknob. Blood was smeared on the green linoleum floor and more blood soaked a dishtowel that lay in the sink.

Calling out her name, Jackson strode to the front door to let Horace in. "Help me look," he ordered. "Don't touch anything. Muriel! Are you here?"

Horace walked to the back of the house, while Jackson pushed open the door to the room adjoining the living room. It was an empty bedroom, neat and orderly, the bed covered with a lace spread. He passed through this room and opened another door, finding that it led to a small bathroom. "Muriel!" he called again.

Then he heard it, a soft moan. He pushed his way through the bathroom into the back bedroom. There, lying in a huddle on the bed, he found her. Jackson came to the edge of the bed. "Muriel. It's me, Jackson."

Her head raised a half inch off the pillow. He saw that her red hair was matted with blood. "Jackson? What…?"

Jackson went into the bathroom and found a washcloth. He wet it and brought it back to her. She took the cloth and began to mop her face. "It's not as bad as it looks, Jackson. I bleed a lot, that's all."

Horace pushed open the door from the kitchen and walked in. "Good God Almighty!" He reached for the phone on the nightstand and dialed 911.

Jackson sat on the edge of the bed and took Muriel's hand. "What happened?"

Muriel raised herself on one elbow, then fell back on the pillow, wincing with pain. Jackson adjusted the pillows, then helped her to a more comfortable position. "That better?" When she nodded, he continued. "Was it Joe Bob?"

She nodded. "He's never done it this bad, Jackson. I've been laying here scared to death he'd come back."

"He won't. Right after we get you to the hospital, I'll have the sheriff pick him up. Now tell me about it."

"I hoped you wouldn't have to know, Jackson. Not this soon, I mean. Truth is, I don't exactly know how to tell you."

"About Ron and you?"

Muriel's eyes opened wide. "You knew?"

Jackson patted her hand. "I'd heard something. Were you with Ron last night? Is that what got Joe all stirred up?"

Muriel nodded.

"Where is Ron now?"

"I don't know. He left. Joe Bob worked him over pretty good, too, I guess. He took off in his car right after."

Jackson felt a surge of anger. "And just left you here?"

"There wasn't much he could do," she said. "I told him to go, Jackson. He's already in enough hot water, what with his wife getting killed. You won't say anything to him, will—"

"Ambulance is here," Horace said, looking out the window. "I'll go let them in."

Muriel clutched Jackson's arm. "Is this going to get out all over town, Jackson?"

Jackson looked toward the door where Horace had just exited. "I wouldn't be surprised," he said.

While the medical technicians loaded Muriel onto a gurney, Jackson picked up the phone and called the sheriff's number. He spoke briefly into the phone, then followed them out to the ambulance.

"I'll see you later at the hospital," he told Muriel. "Right now I'm going to the office."

"Don't worry, doll." Horace patted her hand. "I'll ride in the ambulance with you."

With a grateful look at Horace, Jackson got into his car and drove to the courthouse. Inside his office, he went to a file cabinet and drew out a form from a file labeled *Arrest Warrants*. He sat down at his desk and hastily filled it out in ink, then signed it. On impulse, he went back to the file and retrieved a search warrant form. He was signing his name on the bottom when the sheriff came in the door, followed by Dooley.

"You coming, Judge?"

Jackson nodded and followed the two men out to the sheriff's car. "Do you know where the son of a bitch lives?"

The sheriff nodded. "Been there many times. This isn't the first time that dude's been in trouble." The sheriff turned the car onto Highway 271 going south. "It's in that old trailer park close to Higgins Bottom. You know the place?"

Jackson nodded. "Not too well. We used to hunt

out there as kids. I hear it's built up quite a bit since the packing plant went in.''

''White trash is all.''

Dooley, who was sitting in back, leaned forward. ''It ain't nothing but a cesspool, Judge. Dope and no tellin' what all else goes on out there.''

The sheriff turned the car off the highway onto a tree-lined county road.

''Would you just look at that,'' Dooley said. ''Somebody dumped their trash all in the ditch over yonder. Some people ain't got no—''

''There's the old Simpson place,'' the sheriff said, indicating a broken-down farmhouse where scrawny cows grazed in a partially cleared pasture. ''This is where we turn.''

The sheriff guided the car onto an even narrower and bumpier road. After crossing several cattle guards, they came to the end of the road. There, they found themselves facing an uneven row of mailboxes next to a lopsided sign that read *Peaceful Acres.* Inside the compound, dilapidated single-wide mobile homes were scattered about like children's blocks. The place seemed deserted, yet Jackson had the feeling they were not alone. Once he thought he caught a glimpse of someone peeking through a tear in the aluminum foil that covered the windows of one of the trailers.

''Strange nobody's around,'' he commented.

''Oh, they're here, all right,'' the sheriff observed. ''They just don't like the looks of the car you're riding in.'' He got out of the car and approached a dilapidated trailer with dark brown siding. One corner had been patched with layers of silver duct tape.

Jackson and Dooley followed the sheriff, passing a homemade picnic table that had obviously been used for cleaning fish. Silvery scales covered its surface, reflecting the setting sun, and Jackson could see bits of entrails and bone still stuck to the wood.

"Pee-yew," Dooley said, pointing to a bucket on the ground that held fish heads swarming with fat green flies.

The sheriff pounded on the door and waited. He put his ear against the door, then turned the handle and pushed. The door opened easily enough. "Goddam lock's probably busted," he said. "Joe Bob! You in here?" Then, turning to the others, "Don't look like he's home. Judge, I'm sure glad you went ahead and wrote out that search warrant. Might as well look around long as we're here." He flipped on the light switch next to the door. This illuminated the place only slightly, as the overhead fixture, missing its glass shade, contained only one dusty light bulb.

The room was sparsely furnished, containing only a torn plastic couch and a twelve-inch television sitting on a wooden footlocker. Jackson walked toward the kitchen. A narrow bar separated the kitchen from the living area and was piled with old car magazines mingled with what looked like a year's worth of unopened mail. "I'll go through this." He started pawing through the pile.

"Fine." The sheriff motioned Dooley to follow him down the narrow hall toward the back. "We'll check back here."

Jackson sorted through the mail first, setting aside the magazines as he went. He picked up a stack of mail and fanned it out in his hand. Nothing here but grocery store circulars and junk mail. He put these in a separate pile and picked up another stack, which proved to be more of the same. On the third batch, his eye fell on a half-used pad of deposit slips from the bank. Picking it up, he noticed that it was the type typically used by businesses. Carbon copies were made of each deposit. Jackson turned through the pages of the book. Why would a person like Joe Bob need commercial slips? The deposits, the first dated two years ago, were made on a regular basis, about one every quarter. Most were from a company called J-R-B Trucking. Jackson guessed this was the company Joe drove for. A few were from other trucking companies. The varying amounts, Jackson figured, must represent the length of the runs he had made. The man made a good living. Jackson wondered why he chose to live like this. Losing interest, he quickly flipped through the remaining pages and was about to add this to the pile when his eye fell on a name he had seen before. "Sheriff, come here," he called.

The sheriff came out of the back room, brushing his hands together. "Nothing there but a trash pile. Place looks like a hog wallow."

"Look at this." Jackson pushed the deposit book toward him. "May twenty-first."

The sheriff looked at the page and pursed his lips. "What the…?"

"There's more. Keep going."

TWENTY-EIGHT

WHEN JACKSON came down for breakfast the next morning, Lutie Faye was standing at the stove stirring a pan of grits. Jackson grinned broadly. "You must have read my mind, Lutie Faye. Can I have two eggs with that? Over easy."

"Yes, sir, Judge. Don't I know how you eat your eggs after all this time? You want biscuits or toast?"

"Toast. Where's Patty?"

"Wouldn't get up. I tried. She's supposed to be at her piano lesson at ten. Judge, I reckon you better go up and drag her out."

Jackson grinned. "Be glad to." He knew Patty hated for him to wake her. His method was to stand at the foot of her bed and sing "Louie, Louie" at the top of his lungs until she threw a pillow at him. It never failed to send her into fits of giggles. He went up the back stairs that led from the kitchen to the upper hallway, humming a few bars to get in voice, then, flinging open the door, he went into his act.

The lump on the bed didn't move. Jackson sang louder. The lump shifted, then pulled the covers tighter over its head. Jackson segued into "Bridge Over Troubled Water."

At this, the girl threw back the covers and sat up

in bed glaring at him. Her face was red, and her eyes sparkled with anger. "Please go away and let me sleep."

"Honey, what's the matter?"

"Nothing." She lay back down and pulled the covers over her head.

Jackson sat on the edge of the bed and gently pulled the sheet back. "What's wrong, baby? Has somebody hurt you?"

She sat up. "Yes! You have. You've embarrassed me in front of this whole town, is all."

Jackson suppressed a smile. "That's me, a regular circus clown. What did I do, honey? Whatever it is, I'll stop. I promise."

"No, you won't."

"Just tell me. I can't stop it if I don't know what it is."

To Jackson's dismay, Patty started to cry. He took her in his arms and held her until the sobs subsided.

"It's you and that woman…the kids…everybody's talking, Daddy. I'm so humiliated, I could die." She wiped her eyes on the edge of the sheet. "Could you just stop dating her? Please?"

"Everybody? Who's everybody?"

"Well…Bitsy's the one that told me. But she'll go blabbing it around all over school. I can't stand it. Don't see her anymore, Daddy. I mean it."

Jackson chose his words carefully. "Baby, you don't know what you're asking. I like Mandy a lot. She makes me feel good…happy again, you know. Like I did before your mother died. And, you know, there's nothing wrong with that."

"But Daddy, we were happy. Remember, once you told me I was all the family you needed? Just me and you. Why does she have to come around? I hate her!"

Jackson felt a rising irritation. "Well, Patty, I haven't exactly asked her to marry me. However, I do remember, not long ago, your saying to me that it was time we found you a new mother."

"But not somebody like her. I meant somebody, like, older—like one of the church ladies or something—or Muriel down at the café. She'd be good, Daddy."

"Lutie Faye has breakfast ready." Jackson's tone was even. "You'd better hurry, you'll be late for music."

JOE BOB FLETCHER gave the impression of being huge, although he stood less than six feet. Sitting, he towered over the other men in the sheriff's office. Jackson mused that most of his bulk was from the waist up. His legs were so short and his feet so small that it was a miracle he could reach the pedals on the big rigs he drove. His enormous biceps strained against his soiled white T-shirt, while his head, like a pink bowling ball, rested directly on his shoulders without the hint of a neck to separate the two. He wore black jeans and tiny eelskin cowboy boots. He was talking to the sheriff and Dooley when Jackson walked in.

"It was wrong, Sheriff. I knowed it at the time. But a man can only take so much. Anyhow, I only hit her with the flat of my hand."

The sheriff's eyes narrowed. "Well, the flat of your

hand put her in the hospital and maybe gave her a concussion. Here comes the judge. You can tell him all about how you just slapped her around a little.''

Joe Bob looked at Jackson and tried to smile. ''Hey, Judge. You okay?''

Jackson ignored the question and took a seat slightly behind the sheriff's chair.

''Reckon I gotta serve time for violation of that restraining order you put me under. That's okay, Judge. You got a job to do. No hard feelings. It was just, when I saw her with that feller, something just taken me over like it wasn't even me doin' it. Know what I mean?''

''You've got worse problems than violation of an order.'' Jackson's voice was steely. ''Aggravated assault is a felony. That case will have to go before the district court. In fact, the DA is on his way down here now.''

Joe Bob's eyes narrowed. ''Then I ain't sayin' another word until I talk to my lawyer.''

''Fine,'' the sheriff said. ''Let's talk about something else, then. These deposit slips, for instance.''

Joe Bob wiped his hands on his jeans. ''Lemme see 'um.'' He squinted at the slips of paper. ''I ain't got my glasses with me.''

''Dooley, give him yours,'' the sheriff said.

''Aw, Sheriff. He'll stretch 'um out with that big old head of his.''

''Give him your glasses.''

Dooley reluctantly took a pair of drugstore glasses out of his shirt pocket, which he handed over to

Joe Bob, who took them and began to read the deposit book.

"They're mine." He looked at the sheriff. "Is it a crime to keep up with your own money these days?"

"Not that I know of," Sheriff Gibbs said. "See those pages I've marked with a paper clip? Tell me about those."

"Oh, those."

"Well? Why was Dora Hughes giving you big money?"

"I want to talk to my lawyer."

Jackson, who was letting the sheriff conduct the investigation, now leaned forward. "Joe Bob, did you kill Dora Hughes?"

Joe Bob turned puce. "No! Hell, no!"

"Look." Jackson stared at Joe Bob. "If this money doesn't implicate you in Dora's murder, you've got nothing to worry about. If it turns out to be a lesser crime, I'll talk to the DA. Got it?"

Joe Bob's cretinous eyes turned sly. "How do I know you'll do it? No, I reckon I'll just call my lawyer."

Jackson smiled. "Give him the phone, Sheriff. Meantime, as county judge, I'll just assess the penalty for violation of a restraining order." He looked at Joe Bob. "You understand this offense still comes under my jurisdiction, do you not?"

Joe Bob waved away the phone. "Never mind. I ain't got nothing to hide. This here's what happened. Ten or twelve years ago—no, I guess it was more like twenty—I was driving for Cypress Valley Trucking out of Shreveport. I mostly drove the Rio Grande

Valley route, truckin' produce, mostly grapefruit, but some lettuce and oranges. Shreveport to Houston wasn't so bad, but once you get down past Victoria it's a mighty boring drive—nothing to see but ranch country and after Robstown there ain't nothing but King Ranch and then more King Ranch all the way to the valley.

"Driving through Kingsville one night, I picked up this little old road whore. She said if I'd give her a lift to Brownsville, she'd give me a blow. I said fine, but it 'ud cost her more'n that. She'd have to do it again when I started back. Well, I had a three-day layover down there to get the air brakes checked, and naturally, what with Matamoros right across the border, I forgot all about her skinny self. I gotta say, I was right surprised when I stopped at the truck stop outside of town going north again. I was carrying a load of onions this time. There she was waiting for me. Can I have a cigarette?"

"We don't have any," the sheriff said.

"Water, then."

Dooley got up and filled a paper cup from the fountain in the hall, then handed it to Joe Bob. Joe Bob drained it dry and handed it back to Dooley, who went back for a refill.

"Wellsir, she tells me she's got to go back up to Victoria and she'll be happy to trade blowin' for ridin'. I says fine, and off we go. It went on like that for a year or more. Just about every other run, there she'd be, wantin' to go either north or south and willin' to pay her fare. Then one time...I sure wish I had a smoke."

"Dooley, go up to the courthouse and see if you can find any," the sheriff said. After Dooley left, he said, "Go on."

"Oh, yeah. This time, she was about eight months pregnant. Didn't interfere with her work much. If anything, she was better. And I gotta say, that little gal was powerful good at her job. Well, right after that, I wrenched my shoulder changin' a tire, and was laid off for six or eight months. I'd done forgot about that gal. Then, on my first run out after my accident, I was hauling peaches out of Harlingen when there she is, standin' there at the same truck stop like she'd been waitin' just for me. Only this time she had a baby on her hip."

Dooley came in with a pack of Marlboro reds and tossed them across the desk at Joe Bob, who pulled a lighter out of his pants pocket. He lit the cigarette and looked at it appreciatively. "Uh-huh! Okay, where was I?"

"The baby," Jackson said.

"Oh, yeah. Well, we made the same deal. She nursed that baby, laid it down behind the seat, and we got back there beside it. I reckon that was the best she ever give me—and the last."

The phone rang. The sheriff picked it up and spoke briefly, then hung up and looked at Joe Bob. "The last? You never saw her again?"

"Well, no, sir. I never said that. What happened was, she and the baby rode with me on past Victoria. She had me stop at a roadside park on 59, just outside of town. She took that baby and the little bit of baby stuff she had with it and went into the gals' rest-

room.'' He put out his cigarette and lit another.
''When she come out, she was alone.'' Joe Bob blew
a smoke ring and watched it rise.

''Well, golly, what happened to the baby?''
Dooley's voice vibrated. He had a brand-new baby at
home.

''Hell if I know. She got back in the truck and we
went on. She wanted to go to Houston this time, so
that's where I left her off. At the Southwest Freeway
truck stop.''

''Was anyone else around? At the roadside park?''
Jackson wanted to know.

''Not that I remember. Seems to me like a car
pulled up just as we pulled out. I don't know. It's
been a long time.''

''Interesting story.'' The sheriff picked up one of
the Marlboros and lit it. He had been trying to stop.
''What's it got to do with Dora Hughes giving you
money?''

Joe Bob leaned back in his chair and crossed his
legs. ''That was a funny thing, Sheriff. 'Bout, I don't
know, ten years ago? Something like that, Ron
Hughes came here and went to work for the bank.''

''Twelve years,'' Jackson said.

''Oh. Whatever. Anyway, I'd give up trucking for
a while and went to plumbing. New construction, not
repairs. You couldn't pay me enough to mess with
them shit clogs. Well, they was building up that country club area about then. Me and my boss couldn't
hardly keep up, what with all the work we had out
there on them new houses. One of 'um, I recollect,
was a real pisser. The folks wanted a bidet and a

Jacuzzi and I don't know what all else, all in one little spec-house bathroom. I was sweatin' over how we were gonna plumb the shower when who should walk in but the owners. None other than Mr. Ron Hughes and his new wife. And wouldn't you know it? Miz Ron just happened to be that little road whore I'd known way back when. I opened my mouth to speak to her when old Ron, he introduced her as his wife, Dora. Well, I can tell you flat out, her name sure wasn't Dora then. It was Chrysti. Chrysti Gay. Anyway, when she saw me, I thought she was gonna pass out right there. I winked at her but didn't say nothin'…''

"So, you started blackmailing her," the sheriff drawled.

"Oh, no, Sheriff. It wasn't like that. She gave me money, all right, but it was her idea. I told her I wouldn't tell nobody. I guess she didn't believe me—wanted a little insurance, so to speak.''

"How did it start, then?" Jackson asked.

"Ummm, let me see, now." Joe Bob took another cigarette out of the pack on the desk. He lit it and drew deeply. "Oh, yeah. The next morning, she came out to the job site alone. She begged me not to talk. Said she had got ahold of some money, big money, and decided to clean her life up. Get a new start, was what she said.''

"How do you suppose she got her hands on 'big money'?" the sheriff asked.

"Oh, I know how. She told me. Seems old J. R. B. Starr, owner of the company I worked for, got a look at her. She was real young then, don'tcha know, and right good-looking. He liked what he seen and pretty soon he'd taken her off the road and set her up in a little townhouse in Houston. He even put her in school there so she could learn a trade—a honest trade, that is.'' Joe Bob's lips curled into what might have been a smile. ''Mr. Starr was old at the time, seventy or more, I'd guess. Anyway, according to Dora, when he died, he left her a whole lot of money. A fortune, she called it.''

Jackson got up and paced around the room. How could the woman this man was describing possibly be the same proper Dora he had known? Images popped into his mind of Dora, Bible under one arm, going in to teach her Sunday School class—or Dora instructing Patty on proper table manners. Dora chairing the spring dance at the country club while at the same time managing to spearhead the local United Way drive. He walked over and stood in front of Joe Bob. ''I know you're lying. What I don't know is why.''

''I can prove it, Judge.''

Jackson's pupils widened. ''You're a liar.''

Joe Bob turned to Sheriff Gibbs. ''Take me home, Sheriff. I can show you photographic evidence.''

TWENTY-NINE

ON SATURDAY, Jackson and Mandy rode bikes up to Kinney's Hill for a picnic. Now they lay side by side on a blanket under the trees. The smoke from a wood fire in the distance produced a haze, which blurred the shafts of early evening sunlight that knifed through the branches overhead and splashed onto the mossy ground surrounding the blanket.

"Cold?" Jackson leaned on his elbow looking down at her.

"No. How's Muriel?"

"Better." Jackson traced the curve of her lips with his finger. "She's getting out of the hospital tomorrow. Joe Bob's out on bail, but the sheriff has Dooley watching him night and day. I don't think he'll bother her anymore. I love you, you know."

She turned into his arms and nuzzled his neck.

"Well?" He kissed the top of her head. "You're supposed to say, 'I love you back.'"

Mandy nodded against his chest, then pulled away. She smiled and looked down.

Jackson gave a mock sigh. "I guess that'll have to do. More wine?"

She nodded and he half filled her glass, then his. "I have to go to Austin next week—"

"About the new road. I know. You told me."

"You didn't let me finish. I was going to say, I have to go to Austin and why don't you go with me."

"Can't."

Jackson waited for her to go on.

"I have to give a presentation to the area economic development people next Tuesday." She took his hand and raised it to her lips. "It's something I can't get out of, Jackson. There's something else...I can't tell you now." She looked away.

"Sweetheart, what can't you tell me? Surely you—"

Mandy put two fingers over his mouth. "Hush. I promise, I'll tell you when you get back. Right now it's just not...I'm not ready yet."

Jackson opened his mouth to speak, then snapped it shut. "I guess I'll just have to wait, then." He began loading the picnic basket while Mandy shook out the blanket and folded it. Then they strapped both to the backs of their bikes. "It's getting late." He took her hand and pulled her toward him. "I'm just disappointed you can't go, is all. I know you'll tell me your secret when you're ready."

"You'll be the first to know," she said.

Jackson pointed down the hill. "Hey, see that mailbox down the road? The one with the flag up?"

Mandy nodded.

"I'll race you!"

"You're on!"

Jackson won easily and waited at the foot of the hill, laughing as she coasted toward him, hands and feet outstretched. Reaching out with his hand, he

stopped her bicycle. The two sat for a moment panting and grinning like happy children. Jackson sighed.
"Patty Crain would die of mortification if she could
see us now."

"Really? Why?"

"Oh, you know how kids are."

"Not a lot." She chewed her cuticle in what Jackson thought was a most charming way. "How are
they?"

"Well, Patty says the whole town's talking about
us."

"And that bothers her?"

"A little. What does it matter? She'll come
around."

"Maybe." Mandy pushed off. "We'd better be
getting back."

LATER, JACKSON TOOK the sandwich Lutie Faye had
left for him into his study and ate while he watched
the news. Boston was under a blizzard that had
stranded motorists all up and down the pike. Ice-
encrusted tree branches had knocked down power
lines, leaving hundreds of people without electricity.
Jackson's thoughts went to the crisp fall days the
town had been enjoying lately and thought how content he was to be living here. Texas springs were tran-
sitory but breathtaking while they lasted, almost making bearable the interminable, blistering summers that
inevitably followed. Fall brought color so intense that
it rivaled that of New England, and winter lasted just
long enough and was just cold enough to make the
next brand-new spring ample cause for celebration,

Jackson, comparing it to the seasons of his own life, decided he must be entering late summer. Forty-four. Not that he felt his age. As far as he could tell, his body was as strong as it had always been. Well, he had to admit, not quite. But strong enough. And apart from a gray hair or two, he couldn't tell that his looks had changed that much, either. Now, since Mandy had come along, he wondered if he were not going backward toward the springtime of life.

Jackson was jolted from his reverie when the front door banged. Before he knew what was happening, Patty had hurled herself into his lap.

"I'm sorry, Daddy!"

He put his arms around her. "It's okay, baby girl. Forget it."

"I acted like a creep. I love you, Daddy."

Jackson's heart swelled. "I know, honey. Let's just forget about it. Are you okay with Mandy now?"

She hung her head. "Not really. And I think it's just cheesy the way everybody's talking."

"They'll find something else to talk about before you know it. That's the way folks are, honey."

"I guess." She slid off his lap. "Anything to eat?"

"Sandwiches in the fridge."

As she left the room, Jackson thought about how easy it was for her thirteen-year-old life to shift so quickly from catastrophic to normal. Circumstances that seemed tragic in the morning were all but forgotten by evening. He remembered the child who had been murdered, Boogie. He wondered what problems she had encountered in her young life that had propelled her toward such a violent and brutal end. He watched Patty come back into the room carrying her supper on a plate, saw her flop down on the sofa, one hand automatically going to the remote control on the table. Then and there, Jackson Crain made up his mind that whatever it took, he would see the murderer of that poor unfortunate child brought to justice.

THIRTY

JACKSON AWOKE EARLY on the day he was to travel to Austin. He dressed in jeans and a plaid shirt, then pulled on his old brown cowboy boots. He slung a well-loved corduroy sports coat over his arm and went down for breakfast. Patty was seated at the kitchen table eating cereal. A carton of skim milk was in front of her. Jackson took a bowl down from the cabinet, poured a generous serving for himself, and topped it off with cream. "What's with the skim milk?"

"We're learning about nutrition in health. Daddy, you ought to be thinking about your arteries. You're not getting any younger, you know."

Jackson grinned. "Are you thinking about yours?"

"Uh-uh. This is how everybody eats. It's cool to be healthy. I'm going to start running every day, too. Daddy, can I get a new running outfit?"

"You have to have new clothes to run?" Jackson took a big bite of cereal and smacked his lips.

"Oh, Daddy. Of course not. It's just that some of us girls are meeting at the track every day after school to run together. The boys are having football practice—and we want to look nice."

"I see."

"So, can I? They have some neat stuff at Duncan's. That's where Bitsy got hers—and she said they were real cheap."

"Cheap, huh?"

"Well, the shoes, shorts, shirt, socks, and sweatband cost $67.95. That's cheap, Daddy."

"Okay, go down and get them, charge it to my account." Jackson finished his cereal and put a slice of bread in the toaster. "Want some toast?"

"Nope. I've got to get to school." She turned to leave.

"Wait just a minute, honey. Have you made plans for the next couple of days? You do remember I'm going to Austin, don't you?"

"Oh, yeah." She came and flung her arms around his waist. "I'm staying with Bitsy. Her mom says I can stay as long as I want."

"Good. I'll call you tonight—and take everything you'll need with you. I don't want you in this house alone. Understand?"

The sky was overcast, and by the time Jackson reached the interstate, a slow rain was falling. The windshield wipers did little good against the onslaught of muddy water sent up by the giant eighteen-wheelers as they passed. His shoulders were tight from gripping the steering wheel by the time he stopped for lunch in Waco.

He guided the car off the highway onto Valley Mills Drive and pulled into the parking lot at the Elite Café. He had stopped here often traveling back and forth when he was a student at the University of Texas. The old mission-style building, once an upscale restaurant, had seen many changes in ownership and style throughout the years. In its current incarnation it was done up as a fifties diner with plenty of chrome. Photographs of old drive-ins from that period decorated the walls, and on the jukebox the McGuire Sisters sang "Sugartime." Jackson slid into a blue plastic booth and ordered a club sandwich with a side of fried onion rings.

He had left Post Oak early hoping that he could make it to Austin in time to meet with the highway department officials before the day was over. Now it looked like that was not going to happen. The rain, coupled with road construction, had slowed traffic to a crawl. He glanced at his watch. Almost two, and he was still two hours away from the state capital. Good thing he had had Edna make reservations at the Holiday Inn on Town Lake for one night. He was glad Patty was staying with Bitsy. Still he couldn't shake a nagging worry about leaving her. Until the killer was caught, no woman in town was safe.

It was after five before Jackson inserted the plastic key card into the lock and pushed open the door to his hotel room. He quickly unpacked his bag, then peeled down to his shorts and lay down on the king-sized bed. He flipped on the television to catch the news. Surprising, he thought, so much had changed in this town since he had lived here as a student. Unquestionably, the traffic had increased a hundred-fold. He was surprised by the bumper-to-bumper crunch along the interstate and the large number of subdivisions and strip malls that extended all the way from Georgetown to Austin, replacing what had once been fertile farmland. When he mentioned this to the desk clerk, the gray-haired woman had told him that all this was the result of the high-tech industry now dominating the capital city's economy.

"We haven't changed all that much," she had said with a smile. "We still have a few old hippies left. You just have to know where to look. A lot of them have turned into environmental activists, you know, fighting against development. If you ask me, they're spitting in the wind. You can't stop progress. And we're proud to call ourselves the live music capital of the world. Jazz, blues, rock and roll, country— anything you want on any night of the week, you'll find right here."

"What about The Drag?" Jackson had asked, referring to the strip along Guadalupe Street that bordered the university. "I guess that's changed a lot."

The woman shook her head. "I never go down there. No reason to. I've heard it's full of homeless people now."

"Where's a good place to eat?"

"Depends on what you want." She took off her glasses and wiped them with a tissue. "We've got plenty of Mexican places, most of them good if you stay out of the fast-food joints. Guero's on South Congress is where the president eats when he comes to town. Then there are plenty of restaurants on Sixth Street. Do you know about Sixth Street? It's Austin's answer to Bourbon Street. Colorful. Lots of clubs, restaurants, shops. It's a zoo on weekends when the students are in town, but it shouldn't be too crowded on a weeknight. I don't know. Austin's always had plenty of eating spots. Just depends on what you're hungry for.''

Jackson turned off the television. He wondered if Dirty Martin's was still in business. Jackson remembered hanging out there as a student. The hamburgers had been monumental and almost hidden under a mountain of delicious, greasy french fries. He decided to see.

He quickly dressed in a sports shirt and slacks. It was not dark yet, and the air was warm and dry when he walked out of the hotel and made his way toward his car. Driving west on Riverside Drive, he made a right on Lamar heading north toward the university area. When he turned onto Twenty-fourth Street, he noticed the street was lined with apartment complexes and, farther along, fraternity and sorority houses. At Guadalupe Street, he made a left turn and drove the few blocks to the burger joint.

Dirty Martin's had not changed. It was still in the same two-story square frame building almost hidden by more modern structures. He went inside and seated himself at a wooden booth near the window. A young woman, richly decorated with tattoos, brought him a plastic menu.

Jackson ordered a Lone Star long neck and sipped it while he waited for his cheeseburger with fries. As he sat looking out the window, he saw a group of four teenagers, a girl and three boys, walking down the street. It was obvious these kids were not university students. The teens wore their hair almost shaved. The short fuzz that remained on the girl's head was dyed purple. One of the boys sported a Mohawk and was leading a scruffy dog by a rope tied around its collar. All three were dressed in camouflage fatigues and well-worn Doc Martens. The girl was tiny and her boots looked as if they were several sizes too big. Once again, Jackson was reminded of the girl Boogie.

He finished his meal and ordered another beer. Someone had put money in the jukebox. The music was loud and the words unintelligible. Jackson sat and watched as students with dates, working people, and professors entered and gathered in groups around the tables. Everyone still comes to Dirty's, he thought.

He finished his beer and walked out onto the street. The sun was low on the horizon, but Jackson calculated darkness was a good hour away. He headed south on The Drag toward the university, looking in shop windows and observing the other pedestrians as he went. The desk clerk had been right. Mingled among the students, homeless men gathered in doorways, talking animatedly and gesturing wildly with paper sacks meant to conceal each individual's preferred libation. Later, Jackson guessed, they would all pass out in these or similar doorways.

He stopped at a shaded open area filled with booths offering all manner of handmade items. He paused at a jewelry stand and bought delicate beaded bracelets for Patty and Mandy, then strolled on, passing the old Co-op Bookstore next to a brand-new Barnes & Noble. Farther down, he noticed a three-story square building bearing a large sign proclaiming it to be a church of Scientology. Crossing a side street, he came to St. Austin's Catholic Church. He was thinking it was about time to go back to his car when he noticed, sitting on concrete buttresses in front of the church, the same group of young people he had seen outside Dirty's. They all looked away as he approached the spot.

Again, Jackson thought of Boogie.

He returned to where the teens were and stopped in front of them. "Hey, guys."

They all mumbled an answer, looking at him suspiciously. Finally one spoke. "You some kind of fuckin' preacher?"

Jackson shook his head.

"Cop? We're not doin' anything."

"Nope." Jackson pulled a twenty out of his pocket and held it up. "Anybody ever hear of a girl called Boogie?"

"Boogie-Woogie," one said, doing a little dance step. "Like music, man?"

"No, like her real name's Bougainvillea," Jackson said. "She had a noose tattooed around her neck."

The girl looked away.

The boy with the dog stood up and advanced on Jackson. He was taller and older than the rest. "We don't know her, man. Know what I'm sayin'?"

Jackson, saying nothing, looked him in the eye until the youth backed away. He turned to the girl and put the twenty in her hand. "If you remember anything, I'm at the Holiday Inn Town Lake. Here's my card."

He turned away from the group and walked rapidly back to his car.

The next day, Jackson completed his work with the highway department before noon and walked out of the building with assurances that the matter of funding for the county road would be reconsidered and that the results most likely would be favorable. He had lunch with an old friend, a lobbyist at the capitol, then returned to the motel, relieved that he would be able to make it back to Post Oak before dark.

As he walked across the parking lot, a small figure approached him. "Mr. Crain?"

Jackson saw it was the girl from last night. He took her elbow and led her to a bench under the portico. "You want a Coke or something?"

The girl nodded. Jackson went into the motel and came back carrying two canned drinks. He looked at her. Her dark darting eyes were almost too large for her small triangular face. She reminded Jackson of a mouse somehow, and the image was intensified when she took the chilled can with a hand so tiny, Jackson immediately thought of a paw. "What's your name?"

"What do you care? Hey, you're not gonna come on to me, are you?"

"Nope. I've got a daughter your age. You don't have to tell me if you don't want to."

"It's Michelle, but everybody calls me Missy."

"Nice name." Jackson took a sip of his drink, letting the cool liquid run down his throat, and sat waiting for her to say something.

Finally, she spoke in a rush. "That girl, Boogie? I knew her."

"Yeah?" Jackson waited.

"Like, she's a friend of mine. You know? I don't want anything bad to happen to her. She don't want to go back home. You from Child Protective?"

"Nope." Jackson sensed that this girl was not going to be pushed. Again he waited for her to speak.

"Well, then, what do you want with Boogie?"

"You two good friends?"

"Uh-huh. We went through a lot of shit together. How come you're asking so many questions?"

"Missy, Boogie's dead. Murdered. I'm trying to find out who did it to her."

The girl bit her lip. "I guess I'm not all that surprised. You know? I guess it was Mick did it."

"Who's Mick?"

"The guy she was with. He dumped her, the asshole." The girl drained her Coke. "She left."

"Tell me everything you know about her: where she was from, her parents, friends—anything you can think of."

The girl spoke slowly and hesitantly, as if fearing she was betraying a trust. "She was from down around the coast somewhere. Victoria, I think. Her mom's old man banged her on a regular basis, and she finally got tired of it and left. He beat on her a lot, too, she said."

"Do you know her last name?"

"It was a Mexican name, I think. De something or other. Sounded like Alexander. Nobody pays attention to last names. You sure she's dead?"

Jackson nodded. "I'm sure. Tell me about Mick."

"He was mean."

"That all?"

"He made her get that noose tattooed on her neck. That was his way of reminding her that he owned her. Then, what does he do? He takes up with somebody else. Boogie hung around for a long time hoping to get him back. Finally gave up and decided to get out. Said she had relatives up in East Texas somewhere. She went to live with them."

"Do you know what happened to Mick?"

"Sure. He's at Gatesville."

"State school?"

"Uh-huh. He killed a guy. Beat him to death with a cement block. He'll have to go to Huntsville when he gets eighteen. For life."

"How long has he been incarcerated?"

"Ummm. Six months, maybe? I don't keep up."

Jackson took a twenty-dollar bill out of his wallet. He looked at the girl and added a fifty to it.

"Here you go," he said. "Get some new shoes."

She took the money and turned to go. "Thanks, mister. I hope you find the guy that killed old Boogie."

Jackson watched her leave the parking lot, shuffling across the tarmac in her too-big shoes.

THIRTY-ONE

RON HUGHES SAT on the edge of the coffee table and examined Muriel's face as she lay on the couch in her living room. She was propped up on two bed pillows and covered with a granny-square afghan.

"You look pretty rough, hon." He touched the cut over her right eyebrow. "This might leave a scar."

"What's one more scar? It's the scars on the inside that won't heal," she said.

"Say what?"

"The scars on your heart, Ron. They keep on reminding you you're no good—that you deserve whatever he decides to give you." She pulled herself up on one elbow and took a sip from the glass of tea on the end table beside her. "I s'pose a man can't ever know what it does to a woman to get beat up over and over. After a while, the physical pain doesn't matter anymore. It's the way it makes you feel in your head. Am I making sense?"

"I guess. I just hate the thought that I'm the cause of it."

Muriel laughed a dry laugh. "You? Honey, you're not the cause of it. You were just the excuse this time. Joe Bob's been beating up on me since the week after we married. Any old excuse will do. Once it was because I faded his socks in the wash; another time, I overcooked his eggs. Believe me, you had nothing to do with it. I'll tell you what you did do, though. You came along and gave me the courage to get out. That's what you did.'' She took his face between her hands. ''You be careful. I'm worried Joe Bob might still go after you.''

''I talked with Jackson about it. He says the sheriff is watching his every move.''

''The sheriff doesn't know him and you don't, either. You just watch yourself, you hear?''

''I love you,'' he said.

''I know, hon, and I do you. I just hate I brought you all this trouble. Have you heard anything about the murder investigation?''

''Not a word. The good news is I'm still a free man. I know they'd like to pin it on me, but there's not one grain of evidence I did it.''

''I hope they find the killer soon.''

Ron moved over to sit beside Muriel on the couch. He rested his hand on her hip. ''You know, it's funny. I'm not sorry she's dead. She was an empty shell of a woman, just dead inside. I don't think she had it in her to like, much less love, another person. Dora was as different from you as black and white.'' He kissed her lightly on the nose. ''That's not to say I would have harmed one hair on her head, although I've got to admit, I thought about it often enough.''

She put a finger on his lips. ''Shhh, don't say that out loud. Somebody might hear you.''

''Who? That old cat on the chair?''

''Maybe the sheriff's got my place bugged.''

Ron stood up. "Hon, you've been watching too many cop shows. I have to go. Can I get you anything before I leave?"

"Hand me the remote control off the table over there." She smiled up at him. "You can learn a lot from cop shows."

When the car pulled away from the house, a lone figure emerged from behind the hedge. Without attempting to disguise his presence, he approached the house and stood outside the living room window. He could barely see the woman lying on the couch through a crack in the blind. He stood for an hour, not moving. Finally, the light went out in the living room and the man moved to the bedroom window and watched from there.

"WELL, I NEVER!" Mae Applewaite bustled into the Knitter's Nook, her jowls quivering with indignation.

"What, honey?" Esther was sitting in her usual place behind the counter. She was working on a crocheted baby bonnet.

"The way Jackson Crain is acting lately. It's downright unjudicial, is what it is."

"What are you talking about?" Jane walked out of the bathroom drying her hands on a paper towel.

"Acting like a fool over that Mexican woman, is what I'm talking about. Poor Gretchen must be spinning in her grave!"

"Well, he wouldn't be doing it if Gretchen was here. She's dead, remember? Anyway, I never knew you to be prejudiced, Mae."

"Me? Prejudiced? Bite your tongue, Jane. Why,

there's not a prejudiced bone in my body.'' She took a peanut butter cookie from the tin Esther passed around. ''Remember when I went over to the Negro church and taught the primary Sunday School class for a whole month when Mamie Franklin broke her collarbone? Lord, could those people sing. No, It's just...just...well, there's plenty of nice girls right here in Post Oak he could be going with. That's all.''

Annabeth Jones spoke up from the rocking chair where she was working on the needlepoint kneelers for her church. ''Oh, darn! I think I'm going to have to take out a whole row. Mae, do you think it's serious? With Jackson and Mandy, I mean?''

''When a man's been without as long as Jackson, of course it's serious.''

The others giggled. ''Mae, you're awful,'' Esther said.

''How do you know he's been without?'' Annabeth asked. ''He may have been seeing someone.''

''Of course he hasn't.'' Jane's voice had the ring of finality. ''We'd know it, wouldn't we?''

THIRTY-TWO

JACKSON GUIDED the car onto Highway 183 and headed south instead of north toward home. He was curious about the town of Victoria. Why had its name cropped up so often recently? He had first seen it in Dora's adoption papers, now in relation to the other murder victim, Boogie. To add to that, he was sure Mandy had mentioned something about her family having lived there. What if she was next? He told himself not to be foolish, that it was merely a coincidence. Still, he couldn't shake off this nagging uneasiness. It couldn't hurt to go down there and look the place over, maybe do a little research on the victims. To Jackson, growing up in northeast Texas, Victoria could well be a foreign country. He knew nothing about the town except what he had learned when he took Texas history in junior high. He remembered that it had figured in the Texas war for independence from Mexico. That was about all.

A few miles out of Austin, rolling hills gave way to the flatland coastal plain that extended for miles inland from the Gulf of Mexico. The road signs took on a decidedly Mexican flavor as he passed through the towns of Gonzales and Cuero. Off to the right, he saw a sign pointing to Goliad. Goliad, he remembered from history class, was the town where Santa Anna's men had massacred Fannin's troops at La Bahia, forcing the Texans to draw beans from a jar. Those who drew the white beans were allowed to live, while those who drew black were shot and killed. Colonel Fannin had pleaded that they shoot him in the chest, not in the face, but he was denied even that. The Mexican soldiers raised their guns and shot him directly in the face, then took his gold watch back to Mexico as a trophy.

At Cuero, Jackson turned left onto Highway 87, noting that the sign indicated twenty-nine miles to Victoria. Now the land was flatter still, and live oaks grew low, their branches touching the ground and covered with a peculiar-looking moss that lined the limbs in ball-shaped clusters. On the outskirts of town, Jackson looked at his watch: barely three. He would have time to visit the library before finding a hotel room for the night. He stopped at a gas station with a large palm growing beside it and asked the attendant where the library was located.

"Right that way." The young man pointed south. "It's a white building on the left just as you're getting into downtown. You can't miss it. Big sign."

He pulled into the library parking lot and went in the back door, heading directly for the desk. There he found a gray-haired Hispanic woman stamping a pile of books. She looked up with a smile. "Help you?"

"I hope so." Jackson smiled back. "I'm looking for information on a family, the de Alejandros."

"We have lots of that," she said. At Jackson's quizzical look, she laughed. "Oh, I guess you're not familiar with our region. Don Martin de Alejandro colonized the town of Victoria, although it existed long before he came.''

"Tell me more."

"Be glad to, it's a hobby of mine, local history. Our town has a fascinating past. We go all the way back to Cabeza de Vaca. Know who he was? He first came in 1530.''

Jackson nodded. Here was another name he remembered from his school days.

"It wasn't until 1824 that Don Martin de Alejandro came,'' she said. "He was a rancher in Mexico when he cast his eye on the fertile grasslands of south Texas. He petitioned the government to allow him to create a town on the banks of the Guadalupe River. It was originally called Nuestra Senora de Guadalupe de Jesus Victoria.'' She laughed. "How'd you like to have that name on your letterhead? It means Our Lady of Guadalupe of Jesus Victoria. Guadalupe is the patron saint of Mexico and Victoria was the name of the wife of the president of Mexico.''

Jackson grinned. "Sounds like he wanted to keep God and the president of Mexico on his side.''

She nodded. "Later it was shortened to Guadalupe Victoria and finally just Victoria. Don Martin was the only Mexican national to settle a colony in Texas. Did you know that?''

Jackson shook his head. "Actually, I was more interested in the modern de Alejandros.''

"Then you've got your work cut out,'' she said. "The woods are full of de Alejandros, all descendents of Don Martin. Do you have any more information on the specific family you're after?''

"Not really." Jackson didn't want to tip his hand just yet. "A child was killed in East Texas. We think de Alejandro was her last name, but we're not sure."

"What was her first name?" the woman pressed.

"We only have a nickname."

"Hmm. Not much to go on. I suggest you go down to the courthouse and check the records there. Be prepared to sift through lots of de Alejandros, though."

"I will. And thanks for your help. By the way, can you recommend a good place to stay tonight?''

She nodded. "There's a nice bed and breakfast over on Stayton Street in the historical district. Or, if you'd prefer a hotel, just drive out Navarro or Rio Grande and take your pick. They're hardly ever booked up on weeknights."

Jackson thanked her and walked outside. Standing on the library steps, he glanced at his watch, noting that it was after five. All the county offices would be closed. He took a deep breath and looked at the clear blue sky, larger and brighter than the sky back home where tall trees shielded it from view. He walked back to his car. Since several hours of daylight remained, he decided to explore the town before checking into his hotel. Heading north toward the business district, he noticed that several of the signs on the nineteenth century buildings bore Italian names as well as German and Slavic and Spanish. Farther along, he passed a rather large synagogue built of white-painted brick. He was surprised that this small city, given its limited population, contained such a varied ethnic mix. The store buildings were arranged around a square. A grassy park in the center contained a large and ornate Victorian bandstand. Sidewalks radiated from four of its eight sides to the corners of the plaza. A few people strolled the grounds or rested on green-painted park benches. Jackson parked the car and walked over to an elderly couple seated on one of the benches. The man wore jeans and cowboy boots. A large, tobacco-stained handlebar mustache hid his mouth and most of his chin.

"I'm looking for the courthouse," he said.

The man turned and pointed. "Two blocks over that way. You can't miss it. Stranger in town, are you?"

Jackson nodded. "My first visit. I'm surprised the courthouse is not in the square the way it is in most towns."

"We don't call it a square. To us it's a plaza, De Alejandro Plaza, named after the founder of Victoria County. Have you heard of Don Martin de Alejandro?"

"Just today," Jackson said, "at the library."

"Are you doing genealogical research?" the woman asked. "Because if you are, I'm in the DAR. Maybe I could help."

Jackson shook his head. "Thanks anyway. I'm a lawyer working on a case," he lied.

"Well, good luck, then."

"There is one thing. Could you direct me to a good place to eat?"

The couple offered several suggestions. Jackson decided to find a hotel first and shave and a shower before dinner. He checked into a La Quinta on the outskirts of town. After showering, he glanced at the clock. It was after six. Mandy should be home by now unless she was working late at the office. He dialed her home number and smiled to himself when she answered on the third ring.

"I was raking leaves." She laughed breathlessly. "It's a wonder I heard the phone. Are you coming over tonight?"

"I'm not home yet," Jackson said. "I'm in Victoria…Mandy…Hello…Are you there?"

"I'm here."

"Is something wrong?"

"I wonder why you went to Victoria."

"It's a long story. I'll tell you when I get back. Dinner tomorrow night?"

"I suppose. Jackson…why did you go to Victoria?"

"Mandy, it's nothing. I'll tell you when I get back. Dinner at seven?"

"Call me when you get back. I have to go now."

Jackson frowned as he hung up the phone. Something was bothering her, but whatever it was, it would have to wait until he got home. He swept it from his mind. He would straighten it out tomorrow night. He called Bitsy's house and learned from her mother that the girls had gone to a scout meeting.

The next morning he parked on the street in front of the courthouse and entered the baroque stone building. The county clerk's office was on the main floor and down a long hall. He entered the office wondering where to start first. He spoke to a thin young woman with chestnut hair and prominent teeth.

"I'm looking for information on the de Alejandro family," he said.

"Mister," she said, "you'll have to be more specific than that. This county's full of de Alejandros."

"So I'm finding out," Jackson said. "There was a child named Bougainvillea and possibly someone called Dora, although that may be an assumed name."

She pulled a pad toward her and prepared to write. "Father's name?"

"I don't know," Jackson said, beginning to feel foolish. "Maybe I'd better just start with the birth records."

"Did someone say Bougainvillea? A middle-aged woman stepped up. "I know that family. My daughter went to kindergarten with Boogie. That would be Carlos de Alejandro," she said to the younger woman. She turned to Jackson. "Carlos died in 1990, but his wife still lives here, I think. They had a yard full of kids. Lived under the river."

Jackson's eyes widened. "Under the river?"

She laughed. "That's what we call it. It's a neighborhood down by the riverbank."

Jackson nodded. "I guess I'll start with Boogie's birth records, then. Are they on microfilm?"

"Yes, but that won't do you any good. Boogie was adopted. One of the daughters went off and got herself pregnant and the parents adopted the baby—as if they didn't already have enough to deal with. I'll show you how to look up the adoption records."

She led Jackson into a room off to the side and

explained the filing system for the microfilm records. "That all you need?"

"Are the probate records here, too? I'd like to look at Carlos's will."

"If he had a will, it'll be on this shelf right over here."

Jackson thanked her and went to work. He worked steadily, sifting through piles of paper, making notes as he went. It was eleven by the time he finished. After asking for copies of several of the documents, he thanked the women and returned to his car, a worried frown creasing his brow. He returned to his motel and, after hurriedly packing and checking out, got into his car and pointed it north.

By the time he walked into his house, it was after seven. He picked up the phone and dialed Mandy's number.

"Hi. I'm back. Just drove in."

"Hi."

"You okay?"

"Yes."

"I'm tired, Mandy. Could we postpone our date tonight?"

"Of course. Good night."

He made himself a scotch and sank into his leather chair. The chill in her voice had been unmistakable. He frowned. Where did she get off being so distant? She was the one who had not been honest from the beginning. He sipped his drink and closed his eyes. He had a lot to think over before he came face-to-face with Mandy de Alejandro again.

THIRTY-THREE

JACKSON STOOD NEXT TO the fireplace in Mandy's tiny living room. Strange, he thought, how she had made it her home in a short period of time. The walls, painted a sunny yellow, brightened the gray day, and on a table by the window, a blue bowl spilled over with autumn leaves. Magazines were scattered on the old trunk that served as a coffee table, and family photos lined the mantel, where candles in pottery holders burned at both ends.

She had been furious with him at first and confronted him when he came in the door. Why had he canceled their date? Why had he gone to Victoria? Was he checking on her? But when he opened his arms and looked at her with those Gregory Peck eyes of his, she couldn't stay angry. Instead, she walked into his arms and lay her head on his chest.

Later, she poured tea from a yellow pot and the two sat facing each other on the couch.

"I had to find out," he said. "It was too much of a coincidence, finding that both murder victims had the same last name as yours. And you being so secretive. I still don't understand why you never told me."

"I guess I have some explaining to do."

Jackson waited.

"I am the oldest natural child in a family of seven."

"Natural?"

"Yes. Two were adopted. They had already adopted Dorothea when I was born. She was seven years older than me. Mama thought she couldn't have children of her own, so when the chance came to adopt, she jumped at it." Mandy laced her fingers together and looked at her hands in her lap. "You see, my parents belonged to this Pentecostal church at the time. It was called an 'outreach church' because the congregation was dedicated to doing good works. Once, they sent a group down to a little town on the border and Mama and Papa went along. Poverty is unbelievable down there. Whole neighborhoods have no water or electricity. Raw sewage runs in the ditches where children play. And this is in Texas, Jackson."

"Yes, I've heard," Jackson said. "The *colonias.*"

"That's right. "When they arrived there, my parents discovered a family of eight living in a hovel near the railroad tracks. The children were literally starving. My parents were poor themselves, but Daddy had a job in the oil field and Mama did sewing for people. They brought home this little girl, this little devil, Dorothea." She spat out the words. "You knew her as Dora Hughes."

Jackson nodded. "Go on."

"She was trouble from the first. Mama and Papa made excuses for her because of her background. They thought if they just loved her a lot...but that was never enough. She threw tantrums every day when she was small, calling my parents ugly names— names no child should know. And when she got older, she wanted *things*—you know, things my parents could never afford to pay for." She looked out the window. "Like, well, once she demanded a diamond drop to wear around her neck. She'd seen one on a girl at school. Another time, it was braces on her teeth. Jackson, my parents couldn't afford braces! They had already gone into debt to pay her dentist bills. Her teeth were ruined from the poor nutrition she'd had early in life. By sixth grade, she was re- fusing to go to school. And church, forget it. She ran away all the time, sometimes hiding out for days at friends' houses—knowing my parents were going crazy with worry." Mandy's voice trembled. "Then one day she would just walk back into the house as if nothing had happened. My parents learned not to ever try to punish her because once she had called children's services with a pack of lies. Mama was terrified of losing all her children if the authorities believed Dolo's stories."

"Dolo?"

"That's what we called her back then. Finally, the family just surrendered and let her do as she pleased. One day she left and never came back." Mandy rested her hands in her lap, palms up.

Earlier, Jackson had gone to the sheriff and asked to borrow the photograph Boogie had carried in her backpack. Now he showed it to Mandy. "Do you know who this is?"

Mandy looked at the photo and nodded. "That's Dolo and Boogie."

"Tell me about Boogie," he said.

Mandy got up and poured more tea in both their glasses. She sighed. "Boogie was Dolo's child."

"I thought so," Jackson said. "Joe Bob told quite a story about your foster sister."

"Joe Bob? Muriel's ex?"

Jackson related Joe Bob's story about Dora.

"I guess that's essentially true. We never knew much about what she did after she left home the last time. Occasionally Mama and Papa would get calls from her—usually late at night and usually demanding money. Mama sent what she could at first until finally Papa put a stop to it. After that Dolo never bothered to call again—except that one time."

Jackson waited for her to go on.

"I was in high school when they got the call. She simply told them that her baby would be left at the roadside park outside of town on a certain date and to come get it if they wanted to. Or not. She planned to abandon the baby there either way. Naturally, they went."

"Naturally."

"She was a sweet child—not at all like her mother."

"Ummm."

"But she was high-strung. Know what I mean?"

"Not exactly."

"Oh, Jackson, it just seemed like all her nerves were on the outside of her body. She felt things more than most of us do. If she was happy, she was absolutely brimming over with joy. And funny? She could mimic anybody, and did, whether it was one of her teachers or the clerk at the convenience store on the corner. We thought she might grow up to be an actress or a comedienne. Those were her good days. When she was sad she was inconsolable. And she was impulsive. Once, when she was eight, her friends dared her to climb to the top of the water tower. The firemen had to get her down again.'' She sipped her tea. ''Then Papa died.''

''I'm sorry.''

''It was an oil rig accident. He didn't see the pipe coming. It almost knocked his head off. Mama was strong at first. The doctor had to sedate Boogie.''

''I can imagine.''

''I said Mama was strong at first. Later, she went kind of crazy for a while—started going to bars. That's where she met Ernesto.''

''This is painful for you.''

''Yes, it is, Jackson. You wanted to know, so let me continue. Ernesto was bad news from the first. It's the old story. You can see it on daytime talk shows every day if you care to watch. He beat Mama and the boys. God knows what he did to Boogie. She went into a shell—didn't talk at all for seven whole months. Then, like her mother, she just left one day. After that, Mama kicked Ernesto out and got her life back on track. But we never heard from Boogie again until...until she...''

''When did you find out? That it was her, I mean.''

She sighed. ''I heard some people talking. They said her name—Boogie. I hoped against hope that it wasn't her, but I went to the sheriff's office and he showed me the picture. That was just before you left, Jackson. I wasn't ready to talk about it to you; I had to think. Can you understand that?''

Jackson took her hand in his. "No, dear, I can't. But it doesn't matter. Did you tell your family about her death?''

"Of course.''

"Are they going to claim the body?''

"I spoke to the district attorney about that while you were gone: The body will be released to our family.''

"Mandy, I have to ask you this. Did you know Dora was living in Post Oak when you came here?''

She shook her head. "Not at all. I was totally surprised when I saw her. I don't think she even recognized me—at least she gave no sign. And I had no desire to reestablish any kind of relationship with her.''

Jackson felt a mounting anger. Why had she kept all this from him? He took his hand away.

She studied his face. "Don't be mad, Jackson.''

"How do you expect me to feel? Why didn't you tell me?''

She leaned closer to him. "Maybe shame…maybe fear you'd leave me once you knew my background. I worked hard to rise above that. You'd never understand. Maybe you'd think I killed Dolo—or both of them. We've only known each other a little while, Jackson. How was I to know how you'd react?''

"You should have told me. Besides, how could you possible have committed those murders? They were too brutal. A man had to have done it—a really powerful man.''

''I could have hired somebody.''

''Don't be silly.''

''Jackson, I was going to tell you—eventually.''

Jackson held out his arms and she came to him willingly. He kissed the top of her head and smelled the sweet scent of her. ''I believe you.'' He tilted her chin up and looked into her eyes. ''Just promise me you will trust me from now on. I love you, Mandy. Don't you know that?''

She brushed away a tear with her knuckle in a childlike gesture. ''I promise. So, what will happen next?''

''I think I have to have another talk with Ron. I'll do that tomorrow. Now how about supper and the Wagon Wheel? I could use one of Rip's rib eyes.''

Later, in his study, away from her, his doubts came rushing back. He fought against the suspicion that had nagged him since he left Victoria. Why had she not been straight with him? And what had she really told him today? Certainly she had not explained why she had been so secretive. It was unnatural to behave the way she had. Wasn't it? Two of Mandy's sisters had been brutally murdered right here in Post Oak, and she had never said a word. What kind of person could pull that off? He got up from his chair and took his glass to the kitchen, where he rinsed it out in the sink. Then, turning out the lights, he went upstairs to bed. Later, wide awake in his bedroom, he thought of her again. For all her evasiveness, she had never actually lied to him, had she? He closed his eyes and when he did, he saw her face. Then he knew that one thing and only one thing mattered. Mandy de Alejandro was good and honest and true. If she decided to keep this from him, she must have had a good reason. And Jackson Crain knew he loved her as he would never love anyone again.

THIRTY-FOUR

FOLLOWING ORDERS, he had posted himself in front of the Rice mansion that night. He shivered under his thin jacket, crossing his arms across his chest and shifting from one booted foot to the other. What was he supposed to do here? The orders were incomplete. That was the way it had become lately. The voice, once so crystal-clear, now screamed in his head like a thousand radios in a thousand different languages. He forced himself to concentrate. If he could just grasp one word, hold on to that, then use all his will-power to grab the next, and the next. Maybe then he would remember. If he failed, he knew he was a dead man.

A car drove slowly down the street. He pressed his body closer to the hawthorn hedge, watching as it passed. Dooley Burns in his county car. The man remembered how many times that car had passed while he staked out this house or another, its occupant never suspecting he was hiding there. It was almost funny—could be, if he could only quiet the voices in his head.

What was it he was supposed to remember? He squeezed his eyes tightly shut so that his whole head felt prickly like it had gone to sleep from lack of circulation. Then it all came back. It was the women!

That was his mission. Stop them before it was too late. Mankind was depending on him. Use whatever means at your disposal, they had said. You will be told when it is time to strike. Trust no one. Work under cover of night. Maintain strict surveillance at all times and report any suspicious activities to headquarters. He took a small notebook from his jacket pocket and jotted this down as a reminder. He never knew when the cacophony of voices would launch another assault. Again, he squinted his eyes tightly closed and waited for the brief window of clarity to come. It came, and when it did, he remembered why he was there. Stealthily he walked up the sidewalk toward the mansion, staying close to the bushes. He stopped at the crumbling buttress beside the steps and ran his hand carefully along the bricks. He counted, one, two, three, touching each brick as he went. Number four, that was it. He gently worked the brick from its niche and explored the hollow space it left with his hand, withdrawing a key. Then, slowly, looking over his shoulder, he inserted the key into the lock and soundlessly entered the house.

THIRTY-FIVE

A TEXAS BLUE norther had swept in from the West Texas plains the night before, turning the sky gray and tearing the last, tenaciously clinging leaves from the pecan trees. As Jackson guided the car down his street, he saw Ham Boyd in his front yard with a chain saw, dealing with a limb that had blown down and blocked his front walk. The two men waved as Jackson turned into his driveway. Jackson's hair was tousled from the wind when he pushed open the back door and walked into the welcoming kitchen. Patty was sitting at the kitchen table. She wore one of Lutie Faye's checked aprons over her cutoffs and T-shirt and was poring over a recipe card.

"What's this?" he asked, elaborately sniffing the air. "Have I died and gone to heaven, or is that your mom's gingerbread I smell cooking?"

"Um-hmmm, I'm just checking to see if I got everything right. Sit down, Daddy. I need to talk to you about something." She got up and poured Jackson a mug of steaming coffee and set it on the table.

Jackson took off his suit jacket and hung it on the back of a chair. He loosened his tie. "Something wrong, babe?"

"Kind of…not really, I don't guess. Daddy, I'm feeling guilty about the way I acted…."

Jackson waved dismissively and took a sip of coffee. "We already talked about that. It's okay, honey."

"Daddy, you didn't let me finish."

"Sorry. Go on."

"Well." She traced a finger on the oilcloth. "I've, uh, I invited Mandy to come over for coffee and gingerbread later."

Jackson's eyebrows elevated. "You did? What did she say?"

"She wasn't home. I left a message on her machine. Is it okay? I think I should get to know her better or something."

"Oh, you do?" Jackson was amused. "And what time is this party supposed to start?"

Patty glanced at the kitchen clock. "Ooh! My gingerbread. It better not be burned." She picked up an oven mitt and drew a fragrant pan of the spicy cake out of the oven. "Perfect. Would you look at that?"

Jackson nodded. "Looks just like your mother used to make. Smells the same, too. Now, what time is she coming?"

"In ten minutes. You'd better go upstairs and comb your hair. You look like Larry on the Three Stooges. Oh, there's the phone. I'll get it. Hurry up now, Daddy. Hello. Oh—uh—well…"

Something in her voice made Jackson pause on the stair landing to listen.

"Okay. Yeah, maybe some other time, I guess. You want to talk to my daddy? Okay. Well, 'bye."

Jackson descended the stairs. "She's not coming?"

"Uh-uh."

"Did she say why?"

"She's got plans, she said."

"Was she nice to you?"

"I guess. Daddy, all she said was she's got plans. Okay?"

"Okay. So, she's got plans. Well, here's a plan for us. I go upstairs and change while you cut the gingerbread. Then I'll come back down and we'll pig out. Just the two of us."

Jackson felt mounting irritation as he changed into jeans and a plaid shirt. Who did she think she was, acting like a prima donna? Disappointing Patty? If she had just told him the truth in the first place...

NORMA JEAN GIBBS lifted five slices of crispy bacon out of the black iron skillet and laid them carefully on paper towels to drain. Next, she cracked three eggs into the sizzling grease. Leonard liked his eggs sunny side up with bacon grease tossed over the tops to set the yolks. Last year, the doctor had warned him about cholesterol, but try as she might, she could never get him to give up his breakfast eggs and bacon. She transferred the eggs and bacon to a plate and blotted the eggs as best she could with a clean paper towel.

"You want toast, hon?"

He nodded, never taking his eyes off the paper. "One of these days, I'm gonna take a horsewhip to that Horace Kinkaid."

"What's he done now?"

"He's printed in the paper all about that little dead

girl being kin to Mandy de Alejandro. Now the whole town will be all over it.''

Norma Jean read over her husband's shoulder. ''It's God's own truth. New folks have a hard enough time coming into this town, what with the way people gossip, without something like this coming along. She won't be able to walk down the street without everybody gabbing about her behind her back. Of course, it's not like they weren't already. Her and Jackson, I mean. Hey, I wonder what he thinks about it all. He say anything to you?''

''Now, there you go, girl. You ain't any better than the rest of 'um.''

''That's not true and you know it, Len. I never repeat a thing I hear in this house.''

The sheriff finished the article and folded the paper before tackling his eggs. First he cut them up into a golden, soupy mixture before dipping in his toast. ''Umm, good. At least the sumbitch left out the part about Dora Hughes.''

''Dora Hughes? What about her?''

''Me and my big mouth. Well, you keep your mouth shut about it, you hear?''

After he finished telling her, Norma Jean shook her head in disbelief. ''And Mandy says she didn't even know Dora was living here?''

''That's what she says.''

''What do you think?''

''Could be, I guess. Can I have some more coffee? Stranger things have happened.''

''So, what are you going to do?'' She filled his coffee mug.

"Watch and wait. Stir the pot a little and see what bubbles up."

"That doesn't make one bit of sense, Leonard."

"We'll see." The sheriff got up and kissed his wife good-bye, then put on his hat and left the apartment.

"THIS PLACE IS getting to be a regular Peyton Place." The north wind blew Annabeth Jones into the Knitter's Nook. She carried her needlepoint in a red velvet tote bag. "Lord, it's cold out there." She frowned at Mae Applewaite, who had beaten her there and was sitting in Annabeth's favorite rocking chair, working on her knitting.

"Well, don't blame me," Mae said. "I try to live a godly life."

Annabeth couldn't stay mad long. "I know, Mae. I'm talking about that new woman."

"Now, what exactly has she done?" Jane boomed from behind the counter.

"I guess you haven't read today's paper." Annabeth took out her needlework and held it up for inspection. "How's this looking? I got a good bit done over the weekend."

"Real nice," Jane said. "You expect to get those done by Christmas?"

"Don't think so. Easter, maybe."

Jane, leaning her elbow on the counter, turned toward the back of the store. "Esther, what are you doing back there?"

"Coming." Esther bustled toward them carrying a loaded tea tray.

"Well, tell us, Annabeth. What did you read in the paper that's got you so stirred up?" Jane went on.

"Girls." Annabeth leaned forward. "That girl that was killed? She was her sister!"

The women produced gratifying expressions of shock and disbelief.

"Do you suppose she killed her?" Mae asked.

"Of course not, Mae. The girl was mauled something awful."

"This is not very nice," Amy offered. "She may be real brokenhearted over it."

"That's right, Amy," Jane jeered. "Miss Polly-anna all the way."

"Still...I don't..."

"Well, here's what I think," Mae said in a loud voice. "What I think is, Jackson Crain's going to drop her like a hot potato when he finds out about it."

The others all nodded in agreement.

"Like a hot potato!" Mae added for emphasis.

THIRTY-SIX

VANESSA, WITH AN APRON tied around her waist and a headband restraining her unruly hair, swiped at the stovetop with a dishtowel, then looked with dismay at the towel. A blackish stain almost obliterated the hand-done embroidery on its edge. Lord, she thought, now look what I've done; I've ruined the last one. The towel was from a set of seven her mother-in-law had made her for Christmas last year. Each towel, hand-sewn in tiny colorful stitches, indicated a day of the week. This one was *Tuesday. Wednesday* and *Saturday* had gone in the wash with Steve's red polo shirt and had come out Pepto-Bismol pink. *Sunday* fell into the garbage disposal and was chewed to shreds. And *Friday* and *Monday* had been pitched wet into the bottom of the clothes hamper and left there to mildew. I'm hopeless, she thought, giving the stove one more swipe. She had planned to give the dingy little kitchen a good cleaning tonight while Steve was at the deacons' meeting. She looked around her. Stacks of dishes covered every surface of counter and cabinet doors gaped open. In her early enthusiasm, she had unloaded all the cabinets, intending to replace the shelf paper. Then she noticed the grimy stovetop and decided to start with that instead. Now the whole mess looked insurmountable.

Glancing out the window, she saw that the moon was full and the yard was bathed in its silvery light, a light so bright that the oleanders carved deep shadows on the grass and the bare crepe myrtle trees raised their arms to the breeze and swayed in a ghostly ballet. To hell with housework, Vanessa thought. To hell with Steve. To hell with everything!

She took a sweater off the hook by the door and slipped outside. She pushed her hands inside her sleeves against the chill, made for the redwood picnic table, and climbed to the top. She stretched out on her back facing the sky. I'm miserable, she thought, surprised. I am. I really am! How did I end up here in this pokey little house in this pokey little town married to a preacher I hardly know? What happened to the man I fell in love with? He looks like my Steve; sometimes he even sounds like my Steve—when I make him forget he is a preacher—but the real Steve, the man I fell in love with, is gone, gone to some God I'll never know. And now I hate God for taking him away from me! She looked at the sky, half expecting a bolt of lightning to shoot down and destroy her. I don't care, she thought. I don't want to live anyway. I'm no good to Steve, no good to the congregation, and certainly no good to myself. Maybe I'll leave. Maybe one day, when he's away at one of his meetings, I'll just pack up my things and go. I'll die if I stay here; I know I will.

Vanessa shivered from the cold but did not go inside. Instead, she put her hands behind her head and watched a thin cloud cross the moon. A tear ran down her cheek and dropped on the redwood tabletop.

SONNY SMART PEDALED his bike at breakneck speed down the alley behind Birch Street. He was going to be in big trouble when he got home—and home was a mile outside of town. He was pretty sure his mom would ground him for a week for being late. Sonny hated the idea of being bound to the house for that long, but even worse, he hated seeing the worry lines he knew would be creasing his mother's forehead when he walked in the door. The rule was, everyone had to be home or accounted for before dark. No exceptions. Sonny knew why his mother was stricter than most parents were. It was because she had to raise Sonny and his two younger sisters all alone. His parents were divorced. His dad lived in Galveston with his new wife and brand-new baby. Sonny tried hard not to add to his mom's worries. Tonight he couldn't help it. He had been at football scrimmage for the junior varsity and the coach had kept them late going over some new plays.

A German shepherd barked and lunged at the fence as Sonny crossed under a street lamp and passed behind a large white house. "Shut up, Prince." Sonny knew most all the dogs in town. Prince, recognizing his voice, stopped barking and wagged his tail, but Sonny didn't have time to stop and visit.

Now Sonny was almost to the edge of town. He entered the alley behind the preacher's house, riding fast and breathing hard. His mouth felt like it was full of cotton. Maybe it wouldn't hurt too much if he just stopped by the Largent place and asked the preacher's wife for a drink of water. He propped his bike against the fence and, as he approached the yard, noticed that the light was on in the kitchen. Then he noticed Vanessa stretched out on the picnic table. Just as he was about to call her name, he saw something else. A man was standing behind the oleander bush watching her. Sonny froze. In the moonlight, he recognized the man. It was the man they had seen at the canyon. He saw the scraggly beard, and the wild hair that looked as if it had never seen a comb, the broad shoulders that hunched forward like those of an ape. The man held a tire tool in his right hand.

Sonny got back on his bike and rode fast back the way he had come. He failed to see another figure standing in the shadows.

AT NINE O'CLOCK, Dooley Burns pulled the car into the parking lot at the high school and stopped with the motor idling.

"Where you want to go next, Sheriff?"

"Hell, I don't know. It's a quiet night, you might as well take me on home. I need my beauty sleep."

"Hey, what about me?"

"Wouldn't do you any good, you being such an ugly bastard to start with. You pack it in at midnight if it stays quiet like this. Don't forget to keep going by the Rices' place. I promised the old man—"

Just then, the radio crackled and Norma Jean Gibbs's voice broke through. "Len, you there?"

The sheriff picked up the radio mike. "Ten-four."

"Get over to the Baptist preacher's house. There's trouble."

"That all you got?"

"That's it. Get over there, you hear?"

"Ten-four." He turned to Dooley. "Drive. The Largent house. Move it!"

JACKSON AND MANDY SAT on the porch swing, a plaid woolen blanket covering their knees. An uneasy truce had sprung up between them, born, Jackson thought, out of intense physical attraction along with genuine respect and affection. Mandy had steadfastly refused to talk more about her past, and Jackson had finally stopped asking her. Now, supper over and the dishes washed, they sat in silence, enjoying the moonlight.

The wind picked up and sent a shower of dead leaves plummeting to the ground. In the moonlight, they saw the Boyds' large gray tabby crouch and pounce, carrying away a small twig like a tiger with fresh prey.

"Mighty hunter." Jackson grinned. "You cold?"

"No, but I need to go soon. It's getting late."

"Someone's coming," Jackson said.

"Where? Oh, it's a kid on a bike."

Just then, Sonny shot up the terrace and into the yard, throwing his bike down with a clatter. "Judge Crain!" He ran up the steps and stood before them on the porch. "I gotta tell you something."

"Not Patty?" Patty was at a friend's slumber party. Jackson knew that boys often showed up at these things.

"No, sir. It's the preacher's wife. I think she's in trouble."

Before the words had finished tumbling out of Sonny's mouth, Jackson was heading into the house toward the hall phone. When he came back, he said, "The sheriff's on his way. I think I'll drive over there myself. This guy could be our killer."

"I'm going, too." Mandy ran inside to retrieve her purse.

No one noticed that Sonny had hopped back on his bike and was pedaling furiously toward home.

THE SHERIFF AND Dooley Burns pulled up behind Jackson's car. "Stay low, and stay quiet," the sheriff whispered. They followed him down the neighbor's driveway and into the alley behind the houses. As they broke through the oleander hedges, Vanessa screamed and they saw a man standing over her with a tire tool raised above his head.

"Stop!" the sheriff shouted, and lunged toward the man. Dooley drew his gun to cover the sheriff.

Then, for an instant, a light flashed and an explosion ripped the air, leaving behind a cloud of smoke and the stench of gunpowder. The man dropped to the ground with a gaping hole in his chest. Standing over him, they saw Ray Rice, looking more fragile than ever and shaking like a leaf. He eased himself down on a bench and, almost with surprise, looked at the shotgun in his hand, then handed it to the sheriff.

THIRTY-SEVEN

"RAYMOND WAS A normal boy until he went off to college." Mr. Rice's hand trembled as he lifted his coffee cup. "You remember, Judge Crain."

Jackson nodded. "Ray was a friend of mine."

They were seated in the sheriff's office, Jackson, Sheriff Gibbs, and Ray Rice. Mandy had gone back to her house after staying with Vanessa until Steve Largent arrived to take over.

"He was a smart boy, a natural leader, we thought. He was our only child and a delight to us from the day he was born. Myrtice adored him, spoiled him, I used to tell her. The plan was for him to graduate from Texas University, then go on to get a graduate degree in business." The old man looked down at his hands. "He was going to take over my business."

"What happened?" the sheriff wanted to know.

"Sheriff, I have to tell it my way, if you don't mind."

"Of course. Take your time."

"Ray was a fun-loving boy, unlike me. I've always been serious-minded, as they say. But Myrtice and I, we were glad to see him having an active social life. He pledged a fraternity at the university, Kappa Alpha, I think it was."

The sheriff shifted in his seat but didn't prod the old man.

Ray Rice continued. "He used to bring his friends home from college. My, how Myrtice enjoyed that. She'd clean the house from top to bottom, then bake for a week before they came. When they left to go back, their cars would be stuffed with cakes and pies she'd made. Then, sometime in his junior year, they stopped coming. And his letters home…" He paused. "They became, well, political, I guess you'd call it. Although, I'll admit, we didn't understand his politics very well. He would join various causes—offbeat causes, you might say. This was the seventies, you know, and there were a lot of those around. Student demonstrations, that sort of thing. Could I possibly get a glass of water?"

The sheriff went into the living quarters and came back carrying a glass of ice water. "You can finish this statement tomorrow if you want to, Mr. Rice."

"Are you going to put me in jail?"

"Of course not. We'll take you home. Mrs. Applewaite is staying with your wife until you get there."

"No. I want to tell it all. It was about this time that he started to dress like a hippie. We didn't think much about it. A lot of young people were doing the same thing. It was the letters that bothered us."

"For example?" the sheriff said.

"Oh, he'd take up some cause—like Civil Rights, for instance—and that would be all he could talk about. Then he'd gradually become disenchanted with whatever movement it was and he'd turn directly opposite, virulently so. And for a while, his letters would be full of racial hatred—until he found another cause to support. Finally, it seemed he was against everything. Drugs were a big factor, I think.''

''It happened to a lot of folks,'' the sheriff said soothingly. ''They outgrew it.''

''It wasn't just drugs,'' Ray Rice said. ''It was his brain. Finally, he ceased to function and came back home. It was late in the day, but we finally realized he needed help. We took him to the best psychiatrists money could buy. Every one recommended confinement. The prognosis was bleak. He suffered from paranoid schizophrenia.''

''So that's what happened to him,'' Jackson said. ''His friends all wondered.''

''We never told a soul. You don't wash your dirty laundry in public. At first we put him in a fine private institution. It was expensive, but he seemed to be doing well—even came home a few times for visits, but never for long. I think he really preferred the treatment center.'' He took a threadbare handkerchief out of his pocket and mopped his brow. ''While he was there, the boy met a girl and fell in love.''

''I thought that sort of thing was discouraged at those places.''

''Oh, it was. But, you know, human nature is the same anywhere. They found ways to be together without the staff finding out. He told us about it in his letters, even sent us a picture of her. They had fantasies about getting out of there and setting up a home somewhere. Out of the question, of course, but the wife and I felt it was harmless and it made them happy.'' He took a sip of water. ''Then disaster struck.''

''What happened?'' the sheriff asked.

''The girl's family moved across the country. They moved her to another facility nearer their new home.''

''How did Raymond take it?'' Jackson wanted to know.

''Badly, very badly. He was distraught and tried to escape and follow her. They increased his medication, but it didn't seem to help. Finally, Raymond became convinced that she had gone of her own free will— abandoned him. After that, his letters home started to be full of vitriolic hatred against women. Then came the delusions. He came to believe that all women were Satan's demons. Shortly after that, we had to remove him from the facility. It broke Myrtice's heart and mine, but it had broken my bank account as well. Every cent I owned had been spent on his care.'' He turned to Jackson. ''I know everybody in town thinks I'm an old skinflint. I'm not. Myrtice and I scrape by on our Social Security and that's all.'' He hung his head. ''It's hard for a proud man like myself to admit it.''

''So, what happened to Raymond?''

''Finally, we had to put him in the state hospital. He hated it, but there was no alternative. Then, a few years ago, folks decided that mental patients were better off released into the community—they passed laws. Raymond was released to us, but we couldn't keep him. Nobody could have kept him, because he was free to do as he pleased. And he refused to let us care for him.'' The old man drew a breath.

"Mr. Rice, are you sure—"

"I want to finish. He lived on the streets, mostly. We never knew when he'd appear at the back door, hungry and dirty. Myrtice would bring him in and feed him and give him clean clothes. He would only stay a few days, then he'd be gone again, heaven knows where."

"And this last time?"

"This time was the worst. He had sneaked into the house and was living in the attic for a time. Remember, Judge Crain, when I came to you for help? At that time, we didn't know what was happening, only that something was not right in our home."

"The fire?" Jackson asked.

"I'm sure he set it."

"You should have told us," the sheriff said.

"Yes, I suppose I should. Dirty laundry, you know."

"Did you suspect him of the murders?"

"No, of course not—at least not until tonight when I found him in our house. He was ranting on about something—gibberish, mostly. The wife and I tried to calm him, but it wasn't to be. He stormed out to the garage and came out carrying a tire iron. It was then that I thought of the murdered women, and the whole thing became horribly clear. I loaded my old gun and followed him." He spread open his hands in his lap. "You know the rest."

THIRTY-EIGHT

JANE ARCHER HAD just turned the sign in the window so that the *Open* side showed when Mae Applewaite walked in.

Esther stuck her head out from the tiny kitchenette in the rear. "Morning, Mae. I'm just putting the tea-kettle on. It's going to be a few minutes."

"That's fine," Mae said, taking her favorite arm-chair near the window. "Oh, wouldn't you know it, here comes Annabeth, bright and early. Hurry up, Annabeth. I've got a story to tell that just won't wait."

Annabeth reluctantly took the second best chair next to the tea table. "We all know about Ray Rice shooting Ray Junior, Mae."

"Of course, that's old news. This is something else. Do you want to hear it or not?"

"Wait, I'm coming." Esther hurried in from the back. "Tell us, Mae."

"The preacher's turned in his resignation!" Mae's voice vibrated with the importance of her story.

"Not so," Jane said. "Brother Steve wouldn't do that. I know him probably better than anybody in this town."

"Who says?" Annabeth said. "I know him quite well. When I had the flu last winter, he used to come and sit by my bed for hours. We had the longest talks.''

''He didn't sit with you for hours,'' Jane said. ''Minutes is more like it.''

''Well, he came every day. We became confidants. It's true!''

''He's turned in his resignation,'' Mae said. ''I saw it with my own eyes. I was visiting with Angela Justice. Her husband's a deacon, you know. Well, when she went out to get some cream for my coffee, I saw it on his desk right in their den. Well, naturally, I asked Angela about it, and she said it wasn't supposed to be out yet—that he was going to announce it Sunday at church.''

''What in the world is he going to do?'' Annabeth asked.

''Well, of course, the first thing I did was go right over to his office, but he had already gone home for the day, so I just marched over to his house and demanded an answer.''

''You always were the bold one,'' Esther mused.

''They invited me in and offered coffee, but of course I'd just had some, so I said I'd just have a glass of water.''

''For crying out loud, get on with it.'' Jane tried to hurry things along.

''Well, by the time I left there, I was just so moved….'' She paused. ''Seems the preacher doesn't want to be in the pulpit anymore. He's answered a higher call.''

''What can be higher than bringing lost souls to the Lord?'' Esther asked. ''That's the highest call of all.''

"Not to him," Mae said.

"Then what will he do?" Annabeth asked.

"You'll see soon enough," Mae said. "Now I've got to go. I've got a hair appointment at ten."

ONE YEAR LATER

THE SKY WAS LOW and a bitter wind cut through his suit coat as Jackson got out of his car in front of the Rice mansion and climbed the steps up the terrace that led to the front yard. A thin film of ice covered the water in the birdbath that divided the front walk. Jackson grinned when he saw that all the lights burned brightly and made golden splashes against the dingy stone facade. He crossed the wide front porch and rang the old-fashioned bell. The old place was barely recognizable since Vanessa Largent had spearheaded the idea of turning it into a home for foster children. It was a perfect solution for everybody. Brother Steve admitted that he had become disillusioned with his pastorate and was ready for a chance to serve his God in another way. The Rices, once they became accustomed to the idea, became enthusiastic participants. And now, one year later, it was done.

A girl, about twelve, with mahogany skin and large brown eyes, opened the big door.

"Hi, I'm—"

The girl didn't wait for him to finish. "Vanessa!" she yelled, "Somebody at the door!"

Vanessa, wearing jeans and an old sweatshirt, came out of the parlor. "Tanisha, we don't yell in the house, remember? Oh, hi, Jackson. What a nice surprise. I see you've already met Tanisha. Come in and meet the rest of the kids.''

Jackson followed her into the parlor, which was strewn with boxes overflowing with Christmas decorations. Ray Rice sat at a gate-legged table by the window untangling strands of lights, while, beside an enormous cedar propped against the wall, two teenage boys worked at putting together an ancient Christmas tree stand. Tanisha joined two other girls who were sitting on the floor around a large cardboard box overflowing with ornaments.

"Isn't this wonderful?" Vanessa enthused. "We found all this stuff in the attic. Oh, I know it's early for Christmas." She laughed. "But the kids couldn't wait." She lowered her voice. "Some of them have never had a tree of their very own. Come into the kitchen and we'll have coffee. Kids, I'll be back in a little while. Now, you mind Grandpa Rice. You hear?"

Jackson followed her to the back of the house. "Grandpa?" he asked, bemused.

"I know. Can you believe it? He wanted them to call him that."

She pushed open the swinging door that led from the dining room to the kitchen. Mae Applewaite was standing at the stove stirring something, while Myrtice Rice sat the table peeling apples.

Jackson greeted the ladies, then sat at the table beside Mrs. Rice. "So, how are things going?"

Vanessa poured two mugs of coffee before joining

him at the table. "Well, you know, Jackson, it has taken lots of hard work."

"I can well imagine. Does Steve miss his pulpit?"

"I don't think so. Steve considers what we're doing here, offering a loving home to foster kids, a ministry in itself. As for me, I think it's a much higher calling than preaching—but that's just me."

Myrtice Rice put down her knife. "It has been a godsend for Ray and me." Her voice held tears. "We feel we've been given another chance."

"We couldn't do it without you, Mother Rice." Vanessa smiled fondly at her.

"So, how are the finances holding out? This must be damned expensive."

Vanessa got up and poured fresh coffee. "Mae, why don't you stop working a minute and join us."

"Can't do it," Mae said briskly. "Applesauce has to be watched. Y'all go on talking. I'm not missing a thing."

Of that Jackson had not doubt—and no doubt it would be repeated at the Knitter's Nook the very next day.

"You asked about the money," Vanessa said. "Well, of course you know we used my money to get off the ground. We knew that was not going to last forever. The good news is, Steve has found he has a positive talent for fund-raising and, now he's not begging money for the church till, he really enjoys it. He's in his office now, working on a grant proposal." She got up and went to the door. "Steve! Honey, come in here and say hello to Jackson."

Jackson was surprised to see the once-immaculate

preacher walk in from the hall wearing rumpled sweats and scuffed tennis shoes. "Morning, Jackson. Glad you came."

"Want some coffee, honey?" Vanessa asked.

"Sure." Steve Largent took a seat at the table. He turned to Jackson. "How's Mandy? Have you two set a date?"

"I'm afraid not." Jackson's face grew solemn. "Mandy's not ready to make a commitment."

"You mean right now—or never?" Vanessa asked.

"I'm not sure. At first she talked about giving up her job here and going back to Austin." He looked over the rim of his coffee cup at Vanessa.

"Why do you think she's still here, Jackson?"

FROZEN RAIN had begun to fall. Jackson turned on the windshield wipers as he drove back to the courthouse, passing the Main Street office. Inside, the lights were on. He could see Mandy working at her desk. He sprinted in the side door and went directly to his office, closing the door behind him. He picked up the telephone and dialed her number.

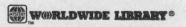

katie's gold

Tom Mitcheltree

When his office and apartment are ransacked and he's
blindsided by an unknown assailant, Paul Fischer realizes
that the saga of legendary pioneer Katie Baker is far from
over! Returning to Oregon's Rogue River Valley to reopen
a case he thought long closed, Paul must outsmart a
brilliant and dangerous enemy long enough to find out
what Katie Baker was so desperate to hide…and why.

Available July 2004 at your favorite retail outlet.

MYSTERY **W(O)RLDWIDE LIBRARY** ®
TM

WTM498

ACTS OF VENGEANCE

FRANK SMITH

Detective Chief Inspector Neil Paget lies unconscious in a hospital bed after an attacker slashed his throat. But the investigation is stalled until a recovering Paget sifts through his tortured flashbacks while receiving taunting calls from a killer who has struck again. To solve a crime that is more personal than he ever imagined, Paget must venture deep into the dark pain of his own past...and the twisted mind of a killer looking for revenge.

"... pleasurable Paget police procedural....
Smith makes this case personal as the audience
gets deep inside the mind of the hero."
—Harriet Klausner

Available July 2004 at your favorite retail outlet.

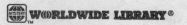 WORLDWIDE LIBRARY ®

WFS499